Classic

WESTERN STORIES

The Most Beloved Stories

Compiled by Cooper Edens

chronicle books · san francisco

May our dreams always be west of here.
—C. E. from the Sioux tribe

Book design by Natalie Davis.
Typeset in Berkeley Oldstyle Book.
Manufactured in China.

Classic western stories : the most beloved stories / compiled by Cooper Edens.
p. cm.
Summary: Stories, folktales, and poems with a western setting, including stories of Paul Bunyan, Pecos Bill,
Indian legends, and tales of Lewis and Clark, among others.
ISBN 978-0-8118-6325-4
1. West (U.S.)—Literary collections. [1. West (U.S.) —Literary collections.] I. Edens, Cooper. II. Title.
PZ5.C5783 2009
808.8'035878—dc22
2008009819

10 9 8 7 6 5 4 3 2 1

Chronicle Books LLC
680 Second Street, San Francisco, California 94107

www.chroniclekids.com

Preface

Us on the Prairie

At thirteen we first saw a railway train, with all the amazing locomotion of the wheels, and the coughing engine, and the heavy clanking bell—a theme for round-eyed wonder. We could ride a bucking pony, cut strange toys out of wood, braid hair or leather into a lasso knot, dive, swim, throw stones, choose mates for bat and ball, and with rifle could behead a quail, such lore folks taught us.

And we whiled long hours of lonely sunshine with our horse and dog, their hearty love dilating soft, bright eyes, pricking glossy ears, their comradeship in quiverings, poisings of graceful bodies, with plain, age-old names like Towser, Flame, Noddy, and Spot.

We learned to read the look and life of all that roamed the wild: Where the first elm seeds showered the April grass; why creatures slipped through thicket, or stirless, hid; where coyotes denned; how lark nest on the ground, two pear-shaped eggs the color of grass in dust, open to sight, so hard to see.

And we knew the frowns and glories of the sky, whether piled thunderheads bridged all the blue, or horsetails waved in the path of wind, or solid gray led up the long, long rain.

We saw the earth arrayed in all its hours; the level sun laugh in the morning dew a-shimmer on each grass-blade, while bare feet were happy in that coolness; we saw the snow dazzling under winter sunlight, shooting a flickering rainbow in greenish eyes.

Sometimes we read the weekly newspaper, and winter evenings helped us into books. On us the Ancient Mariner cast a spell, the Lady of the Lake answered our horn. We struck the proudest blow in Dodge City, linking Kit Carson and Daniel Boone with Davy Crockett, U. S. Grant, Robert E. Lee, and Abraham Lincoln as our greatest men.

—Cooper Edens

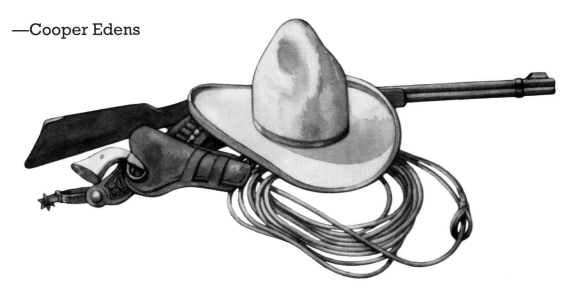

Table of Contents

Western Wagons

By Rosemary and Stephen Vincent Benet

They went with ax and rifle,
    when the trail was still to blaze.
They went with wife and children,
    in prairie-schooner days.
With banjo and with frying pan
    —Susanna, don't you cry!
For I'm off to California
    to get rich out there or die!

We've broken land and cleared it,
    but we're tired of where we are.
They say that wild Nebraska
    is a better place by far.
There's gold in far Wyoming,
    there's black earth in Ioway,
So pack up the kids and blankets,
    for we're moving out today.

The cowards never started
    and the weak died on the road,
And all across the continent
    the endless campfires glowed.
We'd taken land and settled,
    but a traveler passed by,
And we're going West tomorrow
    —Lordy, never ask us why!

We're going West tomorrow,
    where the promise can't fail.
O'er the hills in legions, boys,
    and crowd the dusty trail!
We shall starve and freeze and suffer.
    We shall die, and tame the lands.
But we're going West tomorrow,
    with our fortune in our hands.

Clementine

By Percy Montross

In a cavern, in a canyon, excavating for a mine,
Dwelt a miner forty-niner, and his daughter Clementine.
Oh my darling, oh my darling, oh my darling Clementine!
You are lost and gone forever, dreadful sorry Clementine.

Light she was and like a fairy, and her shoes were number nine.
Herring boxes without topses, sandals were for Clementine.
Oh my darling, oh my darling, oh my darling Clementine!
You are lost and gone forever, dreadful sorry Clementine.

Drove her ducklings to the water, every morning just at nine.
Hit her foot against a splinter, fell into the foaming brine.
Oh my darling, oh my darling, oh my darling Clementine!
You are lost and gone forever, dreadful sorry Clementine.

Ruby lips above the water, blowing bubbles soft and fine.
But, alas, I was no swimmer, so I lost my Clementine.
Oh my darling, oh my darling, oh my darling Clementine!
You are lost and gone forever, dreadful sorry Clementine.

How I missed her, how I missed her, how I missed my Clementine,
Till I kissed her little sister, and forgot my Clementine.
Oh my darling, oh my darling, oh my darling Clementine!
You are lost and gone forever, dreadful sorry Clementine.

Old Chisholm Trail

Anonymous

Well, come along boys and listen to my tale
I'll tell you of my troubles on the old Chisholm Trail
Come a ti yi yippi yappy yay, yappi yay
Come a ti yi yippi yappi yay

Ten-dollar hoss and a forty-dollar saddle
And I'm goin' to punchin' Texas cattle
Come a ti yi yippi yappy yay, yappi yay
Come a ti yi yippi yappi yay

Old Chisholm Trail

I can ride any hoss in the wild and woolly West
I can ride him, I can rope him, I can make him do his best
Come a ti yi yippi yappy yay, yappi yay
Come a ti yi yippi yappi yay

Oh it's bacon and beans 'most every day
I'd as soon be a-eatin' prairie hay
Come a ti yi yippi yappy yay, yappi yay
Come a ti yi yippi yappi yay

Goin' to sell my hoss, goin' to sell my saddle
Goin' to tell my boss where to go with his cattle
Come a ti yi yippi yappy yay, yappi yay
Come a ti yi yippi yappi yay

Goin' back to town to draw my money
Goin' back home to see my honey
Come a ti yi yippi yappy yay, yappi yay
Come a ti yi yippi yappi yay

No more a cowpuncher to sleep at my ease
'Mid the crawlin' of the lice and the bitin' of the fleas
Come a ti yi yippi yappy yay, yappi yay
Come a ti yi yippi yappi yay

With my knees in the saddle and my seat in the sky
I'll quit punching cows in the sweet by and by
Come a ti yi yippi yappy yay, yappi yay
Come a ti yi yippi yappi yay

Old Dan Tucker

By Dan Emmett

I went downtown the other night,
I heard a noise and I saw a fight.
The watchman, he was runnin' round,
Cryin', "Old Dan Tucker's come to town!"

Now Old Dan Tucker is come to town,
Ridin' a billy goat and leadin' a hound.
The hound dog bark, the billy goat jump,
Landed Old Dan Tucker on top of the stump.

Old Dan Tucker went down to the mill
To get some meal to put in the swill.
The miller swore by the point of his knife
That he never seen such a man in his life.

Get out the way, Old Dan Tucker,
You're too late to get your supper,
Supper's over and breakfast's cookin',
But Old Dan Tucker just stand there lookin'.

Old Dan Tucker, he got drunk,
Fell in the fire and kicked up a chunk.
A red-hot coal rolled in his shoe,
And oh my gosh how the ashes flew!

Old Dan Tucker was a fine old man,
Washed his face with a frying pan.
He combed his hair with a wagon wheel,
Died with a toothache in his heel.

Old Dan and me, we did fall out,
And what do you think it was about?
He stepped on my corn, I kicked his shin,
And that's the way it all begin.

Get out the way, Old Dan Tucker,
You're too late to get your supper,
Supper's over and breakfast's cookin',
But Old Dan Tucker just stand there lookin'.

A Song of Greatness

Anonymous Chippewa song

When I hear the old men
Telling of heroes,
Telling of great deeds
Of ancient days,
When I hear them telling,
Then I think within me
I too am one of these.

When I hear the people
Praising great ones,
Then I know that I too
Shall be esteemed,
I too when my time comes
Shall do mightily.

MISS ANNIE OAKLEY,
THE PEERLESS LADY WING-SHOT.

Little Sure Shot

By Alan Axelrod

If any young woman deserves to be dubbed as a Buffalo Gal, it is Phoebe Ann Moses, whose stage name was Annie Oakley. The great Teton Sioux chief Sitting Bull bestowed on her yet another name, Watanyacicilia, popularly translated as Little Sure Shot.

Phoebe's father died when she was six; by eight, she had learned to shoot and helped support her destitute family by supplying game to a Cincinnati hotel. In 1875, the hotel owner staged a shooting match between the fifteen-year-old Phoebe and Frank Butler, with whom she began touring as Annie Oakley.

When Buffalo Bill Cody saw her shoot at the Cotton Exposition in New Orleans in 1884, he hired her for his Wild West Show. For the next seventeen years, she shot cigarettes out of Frank Butler's mouth and dimes from between his fingers. Her skill at skeet shooting was no less phenomenal. Two clay pigeons were released, then Oakley would leap over a table, pick up her rifle, and blast apart both targets. In one demonstration with a rifle, she hit 943 of 1,000 glass balls tossed in the air. In another contest, this time with a shotgun, she blasted 4,772 glass balls out of 5,000 during nine hours of continuous shooting.

Annie's career was almost ended by a train wreck in 1901 that left her with severe internal injuries, but after several operations she recovered and not only resumed shooting but also appeared in stage plays. Although she was born in Ohio and never lived in the West, her marksmanship convinced the American public that she was a true Western girl. Annie died in 1926 at age sixty-six.

The Ballad of Davy Crockett

An excerpt

By Tom Blackburn and George Bruns

Born on a mountaintop in Tennessee,
Greenest state in the land of the free,
Raised in the woods so's he knew every tree,
Kilt him a b'ar when he was only three.
Davy, Davy Crockett, king of the wild frontier.

The Coyote and the Bear

Anonymous Pueblo story, New Mexico

Once upon a time, Ko-id-deh, the bear, and Too-whay-deh, the coyote, chanced to meet at a certain spot and sat down to talk. After a while the bear said, "Friend Coyote, do you see what good land this is here? What do you say if we farm it together, sharing our labor and the crop?"

The coyote thought well of it, and said so; and after talking, they agreed to plant potatoes in partnership.

"Now," said the bear, "I have thought of a good way to divide the crop. I will take all that grows below the ground, and you take all that grows above it. Then each can take away his share when he is ready."

The coyote agreed, and when the time came, they plowed the place with a sharp stick and planted their potatoes. All summer they worked together in the field, hoeing down the weeds with stone hoes and letting in water now and then from the irrigating ditch. When harvest time came, the coyote went and cut off all the potato tops at the ground and carried them home. Then the bear scratched out the potatoes from the ground with his big claws and took them to his house.

When the coyote saw this, he said, "This is not fair. You have those round things, which are good to eat, but what I took home we cannot eat at all, neither my wife nor I."

"But, friend Coyote," answered the bear gravely, "did we not make an agreement? Then we must stick to it."

The coyote could not answer that, but he was not satisfied.

The next spring, when they met one day, the bear said, "Come, friend Coyote, I think we ought to plant this good land again, and this time let us plant corn. But last year you were not satisfied with your share, so this year we will change. You take what is below the ground for your share, and I will take only what grows above."

This seemed very fair to the coyote, and he agreed. They plowed and planted and tended the corn; and when it came harvest time the bear gathered all the stalks and ears and carried them home.

But when the coyote came to dig his share, he found only roots like threads, which were good for nothing. He was very much dissatisfied; but the bear reminded him of their agreement, and he could say nothing.

That winter the coyote was walking one day by the river, the Rio Grande, when he saw the bear sitting on the ice and eating a fish.

The coyote was very fond of fish, and he asked, "Friend Bear, where did you get such a fat fish?"

"Oh, I broke a hole in the ice," said the bear, "and fished for it. There are many here."

And he went on eating, without offering any to the coyote.

"Won't you show me how, friend?" asked the coyote, almost fainting with hunger at the smell of fish.

"Oh, yes," said the bear. "It is very easy." And he broke a hole in the ice with his paw. "Now, friend Coyote, sit down and let your tail hang in the water, and very soon you will feel a nibble. But you must not pull it out till I tell you."

So the coyote sat down with his tail in the cold water.

Soon the ice began to form around it, and he called, "Friend Bear, I feel a bite! Let me pull him out."

"No, no! Not yet!" cried the bear. "Wait till he gets a good hold, and then you will not lose him."

So the coyote waited. In a few minutes the hole was frozen solid, and his tail was stuck fast.

"Now, friend Coyote, I think you have him. Pull!"

The coyote pulled with all his might but could not lift his tail from the ice, and there he was a prisoner. While he pulled and howled, the bear shouted with laughter and rolled on the ice and ha-ha'd till his sides were sore.

Then he took his fish and went home, stopping every little while to laugh at the thought of the foolish coyote.

There on the ice the coyote had to stay until a thaw liberated him, and when he got home he was very wet and cold and half-starved. And from that day to this he has never forgiven the bear and will not even speak to him when they meet and the bear says, politely, "Good morning, friend Too-whay-deh."

Finally, one spring day, the bear said, "I hope you will reconsider our friendship, Too-whay-deh." With a mischievous smile, he continued, "After all, if you think about it, my little friend, you, only you, know my secret. And from now on, you can actually count on me. I'm a trickster, tried and true. Yes, I'm a trickster, through and through. You can trust me. I'll be faithful to you, my little coyote friend. You alone know my true identity. I'm the trickster."

I Ride an Old Paint

Anonymous

I ride an old paint, I lead an old Dan
I'm goin' to Montan for to throw the hoolihan
They feed in the coulees, they water in the draw
Their tails are all matted, their backs are all raw
   Refrain: Ride around, little dogies, ride around them slow
      For the fiery and the snuffy are rarin' to go

I've worked in the town and I've worked on the farm
And all I got is this muscle in my arm
Got a blister on my foot and a callus in my hand
But I'll be a cowpuncher as long as I can

Old Bill Jones had two daughters and a song
One went to Denver and the other went wrong
His wife she died in a poolroom fight
And still he keeps singin' from morning to night

Oh when I die, take my saddle from the wall
Put it on my pony, lead him out of his stall
Tie my bones to his back, turn our faces to the West
And we'll ride the prairies that we love the best

The Cremation of Sam McGee

An excerpt

By Robert Service

There are strange things done in the midnight sun
By the men who moil for gold;
The Arctic trails have their secret tales
That would make your blood run cold;
The Northern Lights have seen queer sights,
But the queerest they ever did see
Was that night on the marge of Lake Lebarge
I cremated Sam McGee.

Home on the Range

An excerpt

By Brewster Higley and Dan Kelly

Oh, give me a home where the buffalo roam,
Where the deer and the antelope play,
Where seldom is heard a discouraging word,
And the skies are not cloudy all day.

How often at night when the heavens are bright
With the light from the glittering stars,
Have I stood here amazed and asked as I gazed
If their glory exceeds that of ours.

Home, home on the range,
Where the deer and the antelope play,
Where seldom is heard a discouraging word,
And the skies are not cloudy all day.

When I Was a Child on the Prairie

An excerpt

By Thomas Traherne

Certainly Adam in Paradise had not more sweet and curious apprehensions of the world than I when I was a child. . . . All appeared new and strange at first, inexpressibly rare and delightful and beautiful. I was a little stranger, which at my entrance into the world was saluted and surrounded with innumerable joys.

The corn was orient and immortal wheat, which never should be reaped, nor was ever sown. I thought it had stood from everlasting to everlasting. The dust and stones of the street were as precious as gold; the gates were at first the end of the world. The green trees when I saw them first through one of the gates transported and ravished me, their sweetness and unusual beauty made my heart leap and almost mad with ecstasy, they were such strange and wonderful things.

Daniel Boone's Last Look Westward

By Humbert Wolfe

To dream of deeds I still have wind to do.
Maybe I have performed enough for one man;
I'm only four-score years, my sons, and a few
To fill the measure up. And so I shouldn't
Be shut here like an old hound by the fire
For there's Kentucky cut from the wilderness
And sewed fast to the States by law and order
Which I'm not saying isn't good for them
Who like pullin' in harness with their neighbors.
But I keep seein' trails—runnin' to westward
And northwest—Indian-footed trails
That no white man has ever pierced an eye through
And beyond them are prairie lands and forests
Which settlers comin' after me could scalp
And sell, if silver is the game they're seekin';
And the Almighty means my eyes to see them.
Else He'd have made my sight dim and rheumy
By now—and where's the deer or bear that gambols
Before my gun and goes away to say so?

It's kind of shiftless maybe, I'll allow,
To want to keep always beyond the settlements
Not in them; ten near families is too many.
But the Lord never meant the plough to be
My instrument: I get to the end of a furrow
And there's the wilderness waitin', all creation,
And I just have to find a path across it
As your ma, there, knows; though I never could tell her
The reason, till they took Kentucky in.
And then I saw that the cunnin' to be wise
With animals and savages was more

Than love of powder and shot; and that God used
My ax to hew a realm out. And there's more realms
Yet to be hewed—and God's grindin' the axes,
I'll tell you that. For, young Lewis and Clark,
Sons of my two old friends, are comin' tomorrow
With unblazed trails of the Northwest in their eyes;
And who knows but that land's as big as Kentucky
And Illinois too; and that they're comin'
For more than to look at an old hound by the fire?
There's one run in me yet; and if I died
Somewhere upon a far new trail with them,
There's coffin-board saved—and I'd sleep better . . .
Unless your ma, this time, wouldn't be willin'
To pack my kit and draw the latch of the door.

She won't, eh? Then it's dodderin' here, I reckon,
And dreamin'. Put on a fresh log, and let be.
Young Lewis and Clark will need a-many like me, though,
Before they hew that Northwest into the world.

California Here I Come

An excerpt

By Al Jolson, Bud DeSylva, and Joseph Meyer

California, here I come, right back where I started from.
Where bowers of flowers bloom in the sun,
Each morning at dawning, birdies sing and everything.
A sunkist miss said, "Don't be late," that's why I can hardly wait.
Open up that Golden State, California, here I come.

Buffalo Gals

An excerpt

Anonymous

Buffalo gals, won't you come out tonight?
Come out tonight? Come out tonight?
Buffalo gals, won't you come out tonight
And dance by the light of the moon?

Oh, yes, pretty boys, we're coming out tonight,
Coming out tonight, coming out tonight.
Oh, yes, pretty boys, we're coming out tonight
To dance by the light of the moon.

I danced with a gal with a hole in her stocking,
And her heel kept a-rockin' and her toe kept a-knockin'.
I danced with a gal with a hole in her stocking
And we danced by the light of the moon.

Oklahoma!

An excerpt

By Rodgers and Hammerstein

O-klahoma, where the wind comes sweepin' down the plain
And the wavin' wheat can sure smell sweet
When the wind comes right behind the rain.
O-klahoma, every night my honey lamb and I
Sit alone and talk and watch a hawk
Makin' lazy circles in the sky.

We know we belong to the land
And the land we belong to is grand!
And when we say "Yeeow! A-yip-i-o-ee-ay!"
We're only sayin' "You're doin' fine,
Oklahoma, Oklahoma—OK!"

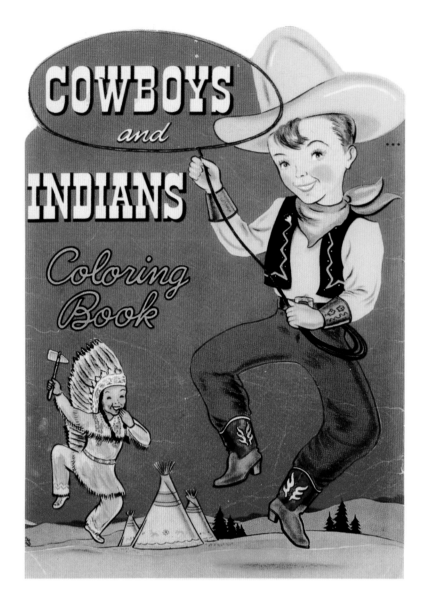

I'm an Old Cowhand
from the Rio Grande

An excerpt

By Johnny Mercer

I'm an old cowhand from the Rio Grande
But my legs ain't bowed and my cheeks ain't tanned.
I'm a cowboy who never saw a cow,
Never roped a steer 'cause I don't know how,
And I sho' ain't fixin' to start in now,
Yippy-i-o-ki-ay, yippi-i-o-ki-ay.
I'm an old cowhand—ay.

Gathering Wildflowers

Photo by Elliott Barnes

Elliott Barnes arrived in the Rockies in 1905 and built his ranch, Kadoona Tinda, on the Kootenay Plains. His passion was photographing scenes from frontier life, frequently using himself or his family as models. This photograph was taken on the Green Spot overlooking the village of Banff.

Tom Mix and the Hoard of Montezuma

An excerpt

By Wilton West

Illustrated by Henry E. Vallely

CHAPTER FOUR

The Old-Timer

It was the fourth day later, when Tom Mix, Shorty, and Betty Calhoun rode into the tiny mountain town of Black Diamond, at the southeastern edge of the Dragoons, and tossed their reins over a hitch-rack before the squat, adobe General Store.

The little town formed the last link between civilization and the heart of the vast, rugged, awe-inspiring mountains lying beyond. Somewhere, far inside, lay the heat-driven caldron known on the Calhoun map as the Canyon of the Lost—a veritable death trap to those who might become lost in its mazes.

Somewhere in the dreaded canyon of desolation stood a sky-scraping, glistening peak, shown on the map, in old Calhoun's handwriting, as "Silver Summit." At its foot, hidden in a cave, placed there long ages ago by the Calhoun ancestors, it was said, in the papers grown old with age, that there lay the great fortune in gold, romantically called the Hoard of Montezuma. The old papers told of prior journeyings of long-gone Calhouns who had tried to find the cache and failed. Some had never been seen again. Into the maw of badlands they had gone, and—vanished.

According to the old map, Silver Summit was formed largely of shiny rock that always glittered in the hot sunlight, standing out proudly, imperiously, luring to death those who tried to reach its base.

As Tom and Shorty swung down from their saddles and tossed their reins over the hitch-rack, Betty dismounted beside them and tied her own horse beside theirs. The beautiful girl

was now dressed in rough range clothes—heavy shirt, stout denim trousers tucked inside cowboy boots, wide-brimmed sombrero that shaded her face, and about her slender waist was a filled cartridge belt and holster, from which a black six-gun butt stuck up.

Tom glanced at the girl keenly, admiringly. Not once had she asked for any assistance along the dusty, sweltering trail. Her seat in her saddle seemed as firm as his or Shorty's.

"Gosh!" he whispered to Shorty. "If she only half knew that we're goin' into. I've been tryin' to make her savvy, ever since we started, but she's sure set hard on comin' along."

"She's shore a plumb good sticker, Tom," he whispered back as he finished tying his reins. . . .

Just as Tom was leading his little group into the store to make some final purchases and get something to eat, a small dust cloud appeared down the lost street. From it emerged a quaint, amusing figure—rather, two of them. One was a man afoot, who was short, squat, muscular, bronzed like an Indian, wrinkled of face, gray of hair and with a stubbly beard and mustache.

The walker's clothes were almost falling apart and covered now with whitish alkali dust. His battered old hat was minus half its brim. His sleeves were rolled high above bronzed, powerful forearms. A Colt's forty-five swung from his ample hips, flapping as he came slowly along.

Close behind him came a shabby, gray burro, its ears flopping grotesquely and part of its left ear missing. A Winchester barrel stuck up from the side of the canvas pack on the little animal's back, while a blackened coffee pot jingled on the pack's other side.

The old prospector halted as he reached the porch, shoved back his hat and grinned up at Tom. His bright, keen eyes twinkled.

The burro halted, its nose against the old man's broad back.

"Hullo, stranger!" the old fellow greeted Tom. "Who be yuh an' whar headin'?. . . I'm Speedy Grimes, jest in from th' Valley o' th' Moon country," he volunteered. Then he mopped his face and neck with a greasy neckerchief. "Shore's hot one, out thar."

Tom saw dried blood on the old man's clothes and wondered about it, but the old fellow continued, grinning:

"An' I got most choked tuh death back thar, this time. I run ontuh a bunch o' five hombres who wants tuh find some place they calls 'Silver Summit.' They choked me hard, thinkin' I knowed." He laughed amusedly and shook his head. "But I give 'em th' slip last night—me an' old Dynamite yere," and he laid an affectionate arm on his burro's neck. He shot an interested glance through the doorway and rubbed his tongue across his dust-covered lips. "But they cleaned me out complete. I had 'nough dust fer all winter."

Tom's eyes studied the old man keenly. His grin became very friendly, for this old man might have news worth hearing—about five men, asking for Silver Summit.

"Come inside an' let's grub-pile, ol' timer," he invited. "You must be some hungry an' plumb dry to th' bone an' ready to eat 'bout a ton."

It was while he, Betty, and Shorty were sitting with the old prospector in the general store, munching canned goods and drinking refreshing coffee, that they gained their first real information concerning Bart Malone and his gang.

Speedy Grimes's story convinced them that Malone and his companions were following the Calhoun map—or trying to.

When Tom finally led his little party outside again, old Speedy Grimes had become an established member, for his knowledge of the Valley of the Moon, near which Tom thought lay the Canyon of the Lost, was remarkable and of the utmost value.

As night slipped down, Tom gave the word and they rode out of Black Diamond almost unobserved. Only the old storekeeper and his buxom wife watched them, for Tom had chosen an hour when he felt that almost no one would be about.

Their holsters sagged now with double guns, while Winchesters were tucked into leather scabbards under their left legs; and from Tom's saddle-horn hung a pair of strong field-glasses in a leather case.

Tom had left Tony, his own horse, behind—for he knew the country he was going into, and now, though he missed Tony's companionship, he was genuinely glad that his favorite mount was safe in corral.

Into the maw of that heat-sodden, rugged country they rode, glad of the coolness of the night. A bright moon helped greatly.

Soon the little group was swallowed up in the wilderness of sand, cacti, rocks and mesquite. Wind, still hot, swept groaningly through countless canyons and down dry arroyos whose bottoms had not known water for years. Sawtooth ridges were everywhere, and rim-rocked ledges—trackless, roadless, endless.

But old Speedy Grimes watched the country with calm, knowing eyes and led the way without hesitation. For thirty odd years this had been his bailiwick, and he knew every tiny water hole.

CHAPTER FIVE
Silver Summit

Four days passed, and still the little group rode canyon after canyon, arroyo after arroyo, crossing country so stiflingly hot and arid that the very rocks seared when touched by naked hands, and the horses shuffled instead of really walking.

Yet Betty rode, climbed or walked, always without complaint, her blue eyes shining with determination, and Tom found himself watching her with something deep and rich springing to life within his heart.

It was only old Speedy Grimes's accurate, marvelous knowledge of the location of the little water holes that made their onward journey possible. This and Tom's own grim determination, for, several times, Shorty and Speedy had urged going back and waiting until winter; and each time that Tom had stubbornly shaken his head he had glanced into Betty's eyes and read there her increasing trust and agreement.

Cowman born and bred, Tom hated the idea of giving up. He spurned the thought. Where other men had been, he could go—and get back.

Somewhere in this void, Bart Malone and his four companions were riding. He felt he had an account to settle with Malone.

Many times they saw tracks of horses, unshod; wild herds roamed here. Cattle tracks appeared now and then, but usually along their way lay scattered bones of the fallen ones.

Old Speedy, however, continued to grin through cracked lips, to chew huge quantities of plug tobacco and to swing his legs carelessly against his horse's flanks.

"We're a-gittin' thar, folks!" he always assured them. "Ain't been travelin' this yere ol' country fer thirty year without knowin' my way 'round."

As dawn broke on the morning of the fifth day, they topped a ridge which gave them an extended view.

Weird, silent, grim, the Valley of the Moon country stretched away, awesome, but grippingly beautiful in its rugged grandeur—a death trap, so it was said.

"We're gittin' plumb clost, folks, now," old Speedy told them. "A short spell now'll see us right on th' spot."

But Tom suddenly gave a low exclamation of surprise as he studied the country below.

To the right front stretched another flat, sandy plain several miles wide; and now, riding across it, going eastward and evidently trying to find their bearings, was a small bunch of horsemen, riding one behind the other.

Tom snatched out his field glasses and lifted them to his eyes. The others watched him steadily, their eyes hard with anxiety. What was he seeing?

Then Tom spoke:

"Bart Malone an' his gang!" he announced. "I'd know that hombre a million miles away. They're ahead of us, but they don't seem sure of their way."

"No," said Speedy Grimes with a chuckle, "thy ain't got me along as their guide— that' why."

As they watched, the Malone gang rode into one of the countless canyons, about two miles away, and disappeared.

Speedy pointed in the opposite direction; so Tom swept his field glasses about in a half circle, and eagerly looked ahead.

They all looked, eyes straining against the glare. About three miles away stood a shining peak with a somewhat steeple-like shape. From it glinted myriad flashes.

Old Speedy laughed as though he saw something amusing.

"I knowed we war shore clost, Tom," he stated. "I been a-ridin' past that ol' steeple all my life, an' never stopped tuh bother." He grinned at Betty's flushed, excited face. "An' every time I rode past it, I been missin' a fortune, huh? Say that ol' peak's nuthin' but made o' wuthless quartz—no good nowheres!"

At a swift gallop, they swept forward across the sandy plain, forgetful of the heat and hot winds.

Fifteen minutes later they swung from their saddles at the base of the towering peak.

Tom was now as eager as a schoolboy.

"A hundred paces due north!" he shouted, dropping his reins and starting off with big strides. "That' what th' map says, folks."

A hundred paces carried them up the side of a steep hill to a winding rimrocked ledge. There they stopped.

Glancing back at their horses, they laughed, for old Speedy had not followed them as they had thought. Instead, he was sitting calmly on a rock, near the horses below, and shoving tobacco into his old pipe. He glanced up and grinned, waving one arm slightly.

"I ain't racin' up no hill after no trick fortune, folks," he shouted up at the others. "I'll stay down yere an' watch our broncs an' packs. Dynamite an' me's clumb too danged many fool hills tuh git loco this time. Ain't no sech think as th' Hoard o' Montezuma."

Tom's gaze shot around. A few yards to his right, a long rimrocked ledge extended, with a huge boulder of many tons against the cliff. He stepped beside the huge mass of rock, peered around it and shouted:

"Right again, folks! Th' cave's here behind this boulder, just as th' map says."

He then stepped to the edge and shouted down: "Speedy, bring up our picks an' shovels. It's here!"

Speedy, moving like cold molasses, did as he was asked.

The three men worked eagerly. Betty stood near them, the field glasses in her hands, for Tom had left her to watch for signs of the Malone gang.

With their picks, they slowly but surely loosened the great boulder from dirt. It stood on the very edge of the rimrock and, once free, would go dashing down thunderingly into the deep canyon below.

A final powerful jerk and it started moving slowly, inch by inch. Then it gathered speed and roared downward with a terrific reverberating noise which seemed to shake the entire mountainside.

Tom glanced around anxiously.

"Them Malone hombres must 'ave heard that, even back as far as Black Diamond, almost," he said. "Reckon we've give away to that gang a whole heap, now. Keep watchin' close, Miss Betty. Th' faster we men work now, th' better, an' then outa here fast."

He darted inside the cave, followed by Shorty and old Speedy. Then all three men stopped, rooted to the spot, their eyes widening in amazed incredulity.

Against one wall reposed a pile of small sacks. Several of them had broken open, rotten with age, and from every tear in the sacks, gold dust had poured. Several nuggets lay on the floor, and there were almost fifty of the sacks, each of the old-fashioned type, about a foot in diameter!

"Holy rattlers!" came old Speedy Grimes's hoarse, wonder-struck shout. He gazed at the pile of sacks incredulously. "Passin' yere often as me an' ol' Dynamite's done, an' only needin' jest 'bout coupla them sacks tuh git me a trip back home! An' tuh think I called this yere ol' Silver Summit wuthless!"

Betty's amused laugh came from the cave's entrance. Filled with eager curiosity, she had forgotten to watch the country and had stepped just inside.

"And where is your home, Speedy?" she asked quietly, her blue eyes shining with warm, sympathetic understanding.

"Brewton, Alabamy, ma'am," Speedy grinned as he hefted one of the sacks. "Ain't been back thar, though, fer forty year, but I'll hit color yit in these ol' hills, one o' these days; an' then I'll go on back thar fer a little spell, an' see a gal."

From below came the raucous gaffaw of old Speedy's burro. The old prospector glanced down. Dynamite was eyeing him solemnly and switching his tubby rat-tail.

Speedy chuckled.

"Dynamite heerd me say that ev'ry year an he ain't got no more faith in that trip or o' me ever strikin' it rich."

Betty stepped quickly forward, lifted one of the sacks and placed it in his surprised arms; then another and still a third. Her laugh rippled out merrily.

"Speedy," she said, "they're yours, and if Dynamite can carry more, take them—and see Alabama. We'll split four ways."

A crashing volley of rifle shots rang out from below. They all dashed for the cave's entrance.

CHAPTER SIX
Miracle Springs

Tom Mix reached the outside first and silently took himself to task for his neglect as he whipped out his guns.

Their horses and pack animals were lying in grotesque heaps, their legs still thrashing about. Even as they watched, the legs sank down, still.

Tom's eyes were wrathful.

"They've sure 'most killed us off, doin' that!" he growled savagely. "Our broncs an' our water an' grub! I'm sure thankful I didn't bring Tony."

He stared across at the opposite side of the rugged canyon, where great boulders furnished a thousand places of concealment, but not a thing over there stirred.

"They heard that darned boulder fall!" he grunted.

The group threw themselves down flat behind rocks. Peering across from keen eyes and with guns ready to blaze Tom crawled along the rimrock from place to place, trying to get a view of whoever had been doing the shooting across the way.

But no movement revealed itself over there, no sounds broke the abysmal silence of the hills.

Yet Tom knew some human rattlesnakes were lying concealed over there, waiting, biding their time.

He finally slipped back beside old Speedy. Shorty was lying only a few feet away, watching the opposite side of the canyon steadily. Betty was standing just inside the cave and Tom caught a glimpse of a gun in her hand. As their eyes met, she smiled and nodded.

"See anything, Speedy?" Tom whispered as he flattened down beside the old prospector.

The old man was chewing hard and fingering his rifle's trigger.

"Nuthin' yit," Speedy whispered back, gruntingly. "But they're shore over thar, waitin' tuh pick us off ef we shows an eyebrow. I heard some rocks over thar slippin'." He looked down at their dead horses and pack animals and spat savagely.

"Them hombres shore know how tuh play thuh dickens with us, Tom, but we ain't licked, not by a danged sight."

"Stick your hat up on th'end o' your gun barrel, Speedy, while I watch," Tom said. "Th' old trick may work one more time."

As the big hat rose, several shots roared out from the opposite side and the hat fairly danced on the barrel.

Shorty's guns flamed at a small spiral of smoke across the canyon. A man's scream rang out. A figure rose from beside some boulders over there and staggered about. The man's arms went flinging out gropingly. Then he

dropped his rifle, whirled dizzily on the opposite edge of the canyon, and plopped out into space.

A second later came the dull sound of a body striking on rock; then silence once more.

"Got 'im, all right, didn't yuh?" old Speedy whispered, his voice filled with admiration as he lowered his hat.

Then the old man gripped Tom's arm suddenly.

"They's an old shack jest a coupla hundred yards back behind us, around th' cliff. I've camped thar many a time. Got water inside, too. Place is called Miracle Springs by us old-timers. I allers keeps a little grub cached thar."

"Then take Miss Betty there, Speedy—you an' Shorty. I'll keep them hombres where they are for a while. Git movin' quick! We gotta be where there's water, an darned soon, an' them fellas mustn't git to it first."

Speedy slipped away noiselessly.

Tom glanced around and watched him as he got Betty and Shorty started and slipped with them around the cliff. The three were crawling flat and thus keeping out of sight of the men hidden across the canyon. A moment more and they vanished from view.

The Arizona Ranger watched the other side grimly. He caught the movement of a man's legs and fired instantly twice—close, but not too close. He wanted to give the enemy something to think about, but he wished to avoid killing if possible.

The legs jerked out of sight and a volley of bullets crashed into the boulders about Tom's head, sending rocky splinters flying. He slipped along the ridge to another vantage point, and repeated the operation.

"That'll keep 'em guessin' as to how many of us are still over here, an' they'll have to come slow," he planned.

Reloading as he crawled away, he finally rose to his feet after getting behind the cliff's side, and raced after the others.

The old adobe shack stood in plain view from where he then was. Flat of roof and apparently very thick of wall, showing the effect of age here and there, the shack, nevertheless, seemed to him a bulwark of protection as he neared it, for he knew no bullets could ever pierce such walls. It stood in the open, and this, too, appealed to him, for no one could approach without being seen from it.

The additional fact that there was a spring inside was of immediate advantage, for no one could live long here without water—not in such seething heat. Besiegers too would have to carry plenty of water to stay long.

Tom watched old Speedy lead Betty and Shorty into the shack and saw the heavy door slam shut behind them. Then he suddenly stopped, for the thought flashed into his brain that the cave stood open now, and the Malone gang could make away with all the gold without further fighting at all!

He whirled in his tracks and dashed back. The opposite side of the canyon was still wrapped in silence and not a figure appeared. He slipped inside the cave and grabbed up three of the sacks and ducked back around the cliff.

At the cabin's door he called. It swung open. He tossed the sacks inside.

"Come on, Shorty!" he cried. "We've gotta git them sacks outs th' cave. Speedy, you stay here with Miss Betty."

The two men dashed back, taking advantage of the rocky outcroppings. Again the opposite side of the canyon revealed no signs of men.

Twice more they made trips to the shack, each man carrying as many of the sacks, each time, as he could handle.

But on their third trip they flung down flat, for now four men were clambering down the other side of the canyon, in plain view, and Tom saw Malone leading them.

Tom's eyes narrowed.

"Four of 'em, Shorty," he gritted. "An' all killers. You keep on carryin' th' sacks back an' I'll do th' scrappin'. Tell old Speedy and Miss Betty not to leave th' shack."

Shorty took another load and slipped away. As he disappeared around the cliff, Tom called out to the men now starting up his side of the slope.

"Malone, if you're aimin' to pass away pronto, just keep comin' up here. High tail it back an' maybe you'll live longer."

The outlaws, at the sound of his voice, leaped behind boulders. Then bullets ripped over Tom's head as they fired.

Came Malone's loud, heavy voice: "We got yuh holed up, hombre. Stick it out up there ef yuh like, but we got yore water bags an' grub an' our own, an' plenty o' time."

For a long moment there was silence. Then Malone called up again. "Come on out with yore paws high, all you people, an' we'll let yuh git your water bags an' grub an' head back for Black Diamond."

Tom smiled grimly. Twice more, as he lay there with tightly gripped guns, Shorty came and went, silently, quickly.

Then old Speedy's voice sounded close. Tom rolled over and glanced that way. The old prospector was lying flat, grinning, crawling slowly forward, his Winchester in his hands.

"I wants tuh git just one squint at them hombres, Tom," he explained in a hoarse whisper. "Shorty's in th' shack with Miss Betty till I gits back thar."

He slid beside Tom and peeped down the hillside. His rifle leaped to his shoulder.

"Lemme take jest one shot at them fellas, Tom. They 'most choked me tuh death!"

Tom scowled. "Remember Alabama, Speedy, an' keep them sacks travelin' fast. We'll have all th' scrapping you want before we're outa here. Them fellas can't move while its daylight. I got 'em stopped. But night's close now. Then we'll have to stand 'em off from th' shack. Work fast an' forget wantin' your revenge against those skunks, till later."

Old Speedy grunted, but he slipped away, and carried more sacks to the shack. Fifteen minutes passed. The outlaws below remained hidden behind their boulders, occasionally driving shots toward Tom's position.

Shorty came and went, crawling on hands and knees.

Finally, Tom felt the young cowboy beside him. He looked around. Shorty's face was pouring perspiration, but he was grinning.

"We got all them sacks down in th' shack now, Tom. Come on!"

The two slipped away behind the cliff, still crawling. Once behind it, they leaped to their feet and dashed for the shack. They darted inside and slammed the heavy door shut. A heavy bar was fastened to its inside, and old Speedy instantly dropped it into place across the door. . . .

CHAPTER SEVEN

Besieged!

Old Speedy was right about the water.

In the center of the room stood the spring—cool, bubbling water! Whoever had built the old shack had done so with the evident purpose of always having his water protected and available. The water from the spring vanished into another hole beside the spring itself.

It was, truly, a miracle spring!

The walls were almost three feet thick and very solid. The roof, however, had sagged away at one rear corner, leaving a two-foot open space.

A couple of decayed, wooden bunks stood against one wall. An old homemade table and a rusty stove stood near another. Two long wooden shelves along one side of the other walls held some canned food and a sack of flour. The front wall had only one window, devoid now of glass and frame, and the heavy door.

Old Speedy spoke as he watched Tom's hasty inspection. "Two-three o' us old-timers has been usin' this old shack fer years, Tom, once in a while. Don't know who built it. I ain't saw th' other fellas now fer 'most a year. They's shore heaps o' yarns 'bout this old place—all of 'em lies, I reckon."

Tom stepped to the window and looked out. It faced the ridge down which they had all come. He leaped aside with a low exclamation.

"They're comin'!" he cried. "They're up on our ridge, watchin' down this way."

Old Speedy swiftly took up a position beside him and stepped before the window, gun held high and his weathered old face grim with his hatred of the gang. Full in the window he stood, for what seemed but a trifling second of time.

A rifle roared outside, from the ridge, and he staggered back, clutching his left shoulder. Blood began spurting through his fingers. Then he began to sink down to the floor.

Tom half carried him to one of the bunks and laid him on it. Betty and Shorty started to pull aside the shirt and bind up the wound—an ugly one through the muscles.

A loud yell came from the men up on the ridge and bullets tore through the window, thudding into the opposite wall.

Tom's hands gripped his Winchester and he ripped back rapid shots at the ridge. But now dusk was rapidly settling down and, almost as he shot, the ridge became a blur. In the east, the moon was rising.

A full five minutes slipped by without any more shooting. Tom watched the ridge steadily, but saw nothing move.

"Reckon they're creepin' 'round out there, tryin' to git closer, Shorty," he remarked to the young cowboy, who was now standing close by. "But with these thick walls, it won't do 'em no good. We can stand them off for a week in here, with all this water, even if we do git kinda loose under our belts after Speedy's grub is all gone. But them hombres will be outa water inside of two days."

Shorty leaned forward, his hands on the windowsill. His head and shoulders, for an instant, were outlined in the window opening, through which moonlight was now coming.

"Mebbe they're crawlin' close ag'in' th' walls," he whispered. "I'll take a quick squint."

He poked his head slightly through the opening, trying to see to the right and left, and a bullet ripped along his right forearm, barely missing his head.

With a low gasp, he leaped away from the window and gripped the arm. But Tom had seen the flash of the gun outside, and his rifle spat twice, swiftly.

A loud, defiant laugh came back from somewhere along the rocky ridge, and several more bullets sang through the window. Others thudded into the heavy door.

What the men outside did not know was that Tom Mix could have hit closer if he had wanted to. Betty reached Shorty and bandaged his arm tightly, using his neckerchief. The cowboy grimaced with the pain, but his eyes held grim fury against the dry-gulchers outside.

Again, as Betty finished, he strode back beside Tom, gripping his rifle.

Tom eyed the wounded man keenly.

"Hurt much?" he asked.

Shorty grunted. "Naw, jest only through th' flesh, dad-gast 'em!" But his hard-pressed lips told another story.

Another bullet came through the window, smashed into an iron pot back on the rusty stove at the rear of the room and sent it flying.

Tom heard a low, quick gasp from Betty, who had returned to Speedy's side. He leaped beside her, lifted Speedy and carried him across under the window and laid him down near it. Then he pulled Betty down beside old Speedy, quickly.

"Stay down, Betty!" he whispered hoarsely. "Nothin' can hit either of you long's

you lie down here against th' wall. That bunk is too much in line with their shots."

As he turned back toward the window, he heard a movement beside him and glanced around.

Betty had risen and was holding one of the rifles, her eyes looking into his flashingly.

"I can fight, too, Tom," she said firmly.

Suddenly, before Tom could answer her, Bart Malone's rough voice came from outside:

"Come outa there, hombres, or we'll shore burn yuh alive!"

CHAPTER EIGHT
Give and Take

From the direction of the voice, Tom Mix knew Malone was standing close against the outer wall and to his left, probably just around the corner of the building.

A rattler ready to strike!

"An' git comin' out one at a time, with yore fingers scrapin' th' sky! We're waitin'. Stay inside there an' we'll boil yuh like rabbits in a pot!"

Bart Malone's tone was savage.

Tom glanced out the window again. The moonlight was almost as bright as day. A rider suddenly dashed by, about a hundred feet from the shack, and drove three rapid shots at the window.

Shorty's guns blazed, and horse and rider catapulted headlong. As the horse scrambled up and dashed away among shadows beyond, it was dragging its rider by one leg. The man's foot had caught in a stirrup. Instantly, more shots came ripping and shining through the window from several directions; again the dull thudding of bullets into the opposite adobe wall filled the cabin momentarily.

A fleeting, dark form rushed past the window and Shorty's gun spat flamingly, but the outlaw vanished, sending a defiant curse. Then again came Malone's voice, but not from the same corner as before. Tom judged the man had shifted positions.

"Let 'em have it, aplenty, fellas!" Malone yelled.

For answer, increased rifle fire came from the shadows beyond.

Tom lifted his Winchester, jerked down on its lever to reload, and the lever stuck. The rifle was jammed! He tossed it aside, leaped across the room and grabbed up old Speedy's rifle. As he did so, a bullet from outside spat across his cheek, bitingly, drawing blood but missing bone. He shook his head to clear it of the shock. . . .

Two shadows flitted from some cottonwoods and his rifle belched swiftly, but the shadows vanished with shouts of derision.

A sudden soft thudding of booted feet was heard outside, near the front door. Then came a heavy, jarring crash against it.

Tom saw the door sag slightly inward. His eyes narrowed into steel points and his lips clamped grimly together.

Malone and his men were using a log as a battering ram!

He whipped up his six-guns, shoved one arm through the window beside the door, pointed the muzzle toward the outside of the door and jerked the trigger twice, like lightning, drawing gun and arm back inside quickly. He had not dared to lean out.

He heard a savage curse before the door, followed by a groan of pain. Then the sounds of running feet faded away. But, beside the outside of the door, the groans continued, mingled with low curses.

Tom looked at Shorty, standing close by.

"Looks like we're cuttin' down them hombres, Shorty," he said grimly. "First, that fella what fell off th' cliff over across th' canyon, then the one what dropped with his bronc over near them cottonwoods outside, an' now a third who seems to be layin' outside th' door."

"Th' only way tuh fight rattlers is tuh give 'em lead poisonin', Tom," Shorty grinned, "or else make 'em danged scared of getting it. An' now that leaves only Malone hisself an' one other," Shorty agreed. "Things is shore evenin' up."

Old Speedy, sitting against the wall under the window, groaned again and cursed to himself. He stumbled to his feet, glaring savagely, and jerked out his guns. Bracing his be-chapped legs widely, he swayed slightly from side to side.

"Dad blast them skunks, boys!" he growled. "Most got me, didn't they? But this yere ol' shoulder's doin' fine now. I kin shoot all right."

From under the window at that moment smoke started rolling up! It swept into the window chokingly, floated through the room and vanished through the hole in the rear where the roof had separated from the walls. They all staggered away from the window, coughing fitfully.

A loud shout of glee came from outside.

"How'd yuh like bein' smoked out, hombres?" Bart Malone's voice roared.

The smoke became stifling. The crackling of brush under the window opening grew plain. Then flames began darting upward.

Tom glanced around the room again, his eyes hard, his brain working fast. Something had to be done and done quickly. The opening in the roof caught his eyes. Darting under it, he looked up.

"Keep firin', everybody," he called softly. "I've got a plan. We've got to get outa here fast. An' you, Betty, stick close to Shorty an' Speedy an' stay away from the window."

Pulling himself up, Tom looked out through the hole in the roof. He could now see down the outer wall; and a man was stacking dry brush against it.

Without hesitation, Tom swung his legs up, cleared the upper edge of the wall and dropped directly down upon the stooping man below. The two men crashed down on the brush.

The outlaw fought hard, but Tom's gun-butt slammed down hard on his skull and the fellow went limp. Tom jerked away the man's six-guns. With a gun now in each hand and his own two in their holsters, he darted across a little open space and into the shadows of some trees fifty yards from the shack.

The noise of the fight, however, had attracted Malone, and Tom, watching, heard the man's heavy tread crushing over the rocky ground around the near corner of the shack, twenty yards away.

Then came Malone's voice: "Git that doggone fire goin' Bull!" he commanded. "Then come back yere in front. We'll plug 'em as they come outa th' door. They're shore coughin' aplenty inside an' they'll bust out pronto or die."

In the shadows, Tom smiled grimly. The man, Bull, could not respond to that order. He lay unconscious from Tom's gun-butt blow, back on top of the brush pile.

Tom heard Malone stride away. He darted to the nearest corner of the shack and peeped around, but Malone had gone swiftly along the front of the house and, a moment later, Tom heard him shooting rapidly at the window.

Tom ran to the front corner and peered around it.

Then he jerked tense and scowled. Malone was now kneeling behind a big rock, his back toward him, and was banging away at the shack with a rifle. Close in front of the door, a man was slowly rising, guns in hand and cursing savagely.

Tom watched. He heard heavy coughing coming from inside the building and saw burning brush flaming high under the window. Then the man by the door joined Malone and both fired at the window.

From inside the shack, shots rang out as those inside drove lead at the two outlaws.

Tom moved warily forward on tiptoes, gripping a six-gun in each hand, until he was within ten feet of the two outlaws. Then he coolly waited, a grim smile on his blood smeared face.

The two men's firing stopped a moment later and they both started reloading their guns.

Tom's moment had arrived! Reversing one gun, he leaped forward and crashed its butt down on the head of the man lying beside Malone. The fellow flattened with a deep groan and lay unconscious.

Malone whirled and leaped to his feet, his face filled with astounded perplexity. Then his guns shot upward and the hammers clicked down—on empty chambers! . . . Malone slammed one of his useless guns savagely at Tom's face. Tom ducked and leaped straight at him. His own gun swept in a short circle for Malone's head, but the huge, gorilla-like man side-stepped and gripped Tom's gun-wrist like a vise. Malone's massive fist struck against Tom's ribs. Tom felt as if his side had been crushed in, but he drove in a terrific left to Malone's mouth and nose.

From the window came Shorty's choking voice through the thick outpouring smoke: "That you out there, Tom?" it shouted.

"Yeah, Shorty, don't shoot!" Tom yelled back. "Throw open th' door an' come on out."

At Tom's words, Malone ripped out a savage oath and rushed at him again, but once more Tom's fists slammed out and reached the outlaw's chin.

Malone reeled back, drunkenly. Another staggering blow from Tom landed squarely against Malone's throat, and the outlaw shot backward with a hoarse, choking gasp. On his back, ten feet away, he went limp.

Tom darted beside him, fists clenched, but Malone lay with closed, battered eyes, unconscious. In falling, his head had crashed with terrific force against a boulder.

"Look out, Tom—behind you!" came Shorty's yell.

Tom instantly dropped flat. A rifle shot roared and he was conscious of a big form pitching headlong just behind him. He rolled over and looked. Shorty was coming forward, smoke curling up from the muzzle of his Winchester, and behind him came Betty and old Speedy.

Tom looked around at the prone figure that had just fallen behind him. It was the man whom he had struck down beside Malone. Blood was slowly oozing from the outlaw's head. The fellow was dead.

"He was jest about to bore you with his gun, Tom," Shorty stated grimly, "so I let 'im have it, quick."

"An' saved my life, Shorty!" Tom replied.

CHAPTER NINE
Toll

Tom Mix and Shorty roped the outlaw's hands behind his back. Then, to make doubly sure, they roped his ankles.

But as Tom rose, he staggered dizzily and rubbed a hand across his battered eyes. Malone had landed some mighty blows against them, and things began swimming before him, crazily. His side felt as if it was splitting open. His breathing sent cutting pains along his ribs. Suddenly he sat down on Malone's body and wagged his head from side to side. That blow in the ribs which Malone had driven home had not seemed so much at the moment, but now its after-effects were gripping those ribs like steel teeth.

He felt himself drifting away. Then he was conscious of Betty's arms about him, heard her voice dimly, and old Speedy's, but the voices were indistinct, as if far away.

"Find their hosses, quick!" he mumbled. "Our only chance to get outa this—"

He sank lower, gasping for breath. Confusion was sweeping over his brain. His lips mumbled, incoherently.

"Silver Summit—Alabama—th' Canyon o' th' Lost—Black Diamond, gotta git there an'—hole in th' roof—Malone, yore down an'—"

Then his world went blank.

When Tom next opened his eyes, he was lying on one of the bunks. Betty, Shorty, and old Speedy were sitting near him. A tight bandage around his ribs allowed him to breathe without that racking pain.

He gazed around in a daze.

Bright sunlight was streaming through the open doorway. Then he suddenly tensed, for Bart Malone's body, on its back, was lying outside under a tree, in plain view from the shack, and without ropes! Tom half rose, but he sank back as another sharp pain darted through his side.

"Malone's out there, loose!" he cried.

Old Speedy's gruff voice answered soberly: "That hombre ain't needin' no more ropes, Tom. His durned head busted when it struck ag'in' that boulder, after yuh'd give 'im that poke in th' throat. He passed away last night, while you was layin' yere unconscious."

Speedy's big hand touched Tom's shoulder affectionately.

"But you keep layin' still, yuh durned young fightin' rannihan. He 'most drove yore ribs through yore back. So fur as we kin tell, yuh've got 'bout three busted, looks like."

"What about them other outlaws layin' outside, Speedy?" Tom asked. "Th' one that fell from th' cliff, an' th' fella what was bein' dragged by his bronc, an' that hombre I banged over th' head on th' brush pile below th' hole in th' roof?"

"Don't git doin' no worrying 'bout them fellas, son," old Speedy growled. "We've took a look around at 'em. Th' cliff jumper's dead, layin' there among th' rocks. Th' one what was bein' dragged may still be travelin' in that durned stirrup. We ain't seen 'im or his bronc since. An' th' one what yuh slammed over th' cabesa at the pile o' brush is roped hawg-tight outside. We are takin' 'im back with us. He's confessed one heap o' things what'd make any sheriff hang 'im on sight. . . ."

Tom grinned and smoothed one hand over the Ranger badge on his left breast.

"A Ranger's supposed tuh git his men alive, when he can," he said, "but looks like I'll only be takin' one back thataway this time."

He eyed a bandage that was around old Speedy's shoulder. It was revealing signs of blood underneath. Then he saw a bandage around Shorty's forearm, also somewhat bloody.

"Reckon us three fellas'll all bear brands as long as we live, eh, but got honest an' in th' name o' th' law." He rubbed his hand across his face, where that bullet had scraped across his cheek, leaving an ugly wound in the skin. But the bleeding, under the combined care of Shorty, Betty, and old Speedy while he had lain unconscious, had been stopped.

"How's yore shoulder, Speedy?"

"Fine, fine, Tom," the old prospector assured him, with a grin. "Only got me through th' flesh. Sorta stiff, but I kin fight a grizzly fer money, chalk, or marbles, any time!"

"An' how's that arm o' yours, Shorty?" Tom asked.

"Pshaw, Tom!" the young cowboy laughed. "I've had worse. 'Taint nothin' worth mentionin'. Fergit it."

Betty lifted Tom's head and held a tin cup of cool water against his hot lips. He drank thirstily, smiling his gratitude. Then he sat up and swung his legs, in chaps as always, over the edge of the old bunk and pulled on his high-heeled boots.

"Well, folks," he said, "I guess everything's all over but th' shoutin', an' Miss Betty's got her Hoard o' Montezuma at last."

He rose slowly to his feet and found that his strength had flowed back wonderfully.

"We've cleaned out one o' th' toughest gangs what ever rode this border," he added. Then he studied Betty keenly, admiringly. "An' you've gone through aplenty an' then some, Miss Betty. We take our Stetsons off to you. Now, folks, we've gotta get outs here an' back to Black Diamond with them gold sacs. Never no tellin', in these blazin' badlands, when some more renegades'll come rompin' around. An' besides, th' Gov'nor, who sent me down to Miss Betty's Red Rock Ranch to help her father out, will be wonderin' what's become o' me an' he'll be wantin' my official report. Let's start packin' out o' here."

CHAPTER TEN
Divided Four Ways

Three days more went by before Tom's side, old Speedy's shoulder and Shorty's arm were well enough for them to make the start. Then, driving the heavily loaded pack animals before them, and with their prisoner roped to his saddle and Betty riding behind the man and carrying a loaded six-gun well forward on her right hip if he should attempt a break as the other three herded the pack, they headed back across the wild badlands, under the scorching sun, for Black Diamond.

Due to old Speedy's intimate knowledge of the country and of the locations of the water holes, they were able to make several shortcuts.

Even then it was sundown of the seventh day before they rode into the dusty streets of Black Diamond, ragged, dust-soaked, begrimed of face and reddened of eyes from the glare of blazing suns on yellow sand.

They turned their lone prisoner over to the sheriff.

The people of the little cowtown quickly gathered about them, listening intently

as they related their story. Two hours later, the town's sheriff and a posse, with a copy of Betty's map, rode away for Silver Summit and the outlaws' bodies.

A few days later, the sacks of gold had been safely deposited in the bank in Rawhide, ten miles north of Betty's home. Tom, Shorty, and old Speedy stood on her wide porch and watched the sunset with her. The depositing of the Hoard of Montezuma had been made under Betty's personal and firm direction.

"It must be just this way, boys," she had said, and no protests from them had been able to alter her decision. "We now have wealth enough for us all, and each of us shall take a fourth."

In this way the Hoard of Montezuma was deposited a quarter to the credit of each.

Now, as they stood watching the sunset, Tom grinned around at them. A chuckle came from his lips.

"Yes, sir, folks," he said, "all this new wealth is shore gonna destroy us three waddies. Old Speedy here'll be ridin' back to Alabama in one o' them plush-covered pullmans, come noon tomorrow, an' expects tuh find his old yaller-haired gall o' forty years ago waitin' to hug 'im at th' station back in his Brewton, an'—"

Old Speedy banged him across his back and eyed him fiercely. Then his reply roared: "She ain't yaller-haired, not never, yuh locoed young buckaroo. Her hair's brown, allers was, an' it warn't forty years ago. She's still young. It was only thirty-eight years since I been there an' seen 'er."

"An' Shorty here," Tom laughed as he hugged old Speedy close, "he'll be splicin' up with his black-eyed Lucy up in Rawhide an' relievin' her o' all th' cookin' she's been doin' up in Ma Bunker's restaurant an' getting' up at four a.m. to milk th' hotel's cows."

"Yeah, that's what you say!" Shorty snorted. "Well, seein' yore so durned set on arrangin' our futures, Mister Mixer, listen good. Lucy's eyes is as blue as Miss Betty's yere, an' she ain't cookin' fer Ma Bunker no more. We was married last evenin' an' we've done hired th' old Milligan ranch, so that's where you git off."

Then his eyes softened with affection as he looked at Tom.

"An' they's allers one special room we're gonna set aside jest fer you, Tom. Yuh can't come too soon nor stay too long. Yuh knows that."

Their hands gripped.

"And—and—you, Tom?" Betty asked, her eyes suddenly grown slightly misty.

They had never held a deeper or bluer light as they met his.

For once he stammered and his fingers started twisting his hat brim as he swung the Stetson against his chaps.

"Why—why—er, Betty, I—I—er—sorta was figgerin' on askin' yuh tuh let me buy a half interest in th' ranch here an'—an'—be yore pardner."

"Yes, Tom, I'd like that," Betty answered softly.

Tom suddenly whirled on old Speedy and Shorty.

"Here, you two doggoned worthless bronc peelers, git on down tuh Miss Betty's barn an' milk them cows o' hers. I ain't never knowed two such lazy mortals since I was—"

But by then old Speedy and Shorty were jumping from the porch and scooting for the barn. Once there, Shorty leaned close to old Speedy's left ear and whispered: "Thinks he's ownin' the place, wouldn't yuh say, old timer?"

Old Speedy spat and then eyed him scowlingly and snorted, "If he do or don't, we'll take his orders an' like 'em. Never was a finer all-round man, if yuh asks me."

Mamas, Don't Let Your Babies Grow Up to Be Cowboys

An excerpt

By Ed and Patsy Bruce

Cowboys ain't easy to love and they're harder to hold
They'd rather give you a song than diamonds or gold
Lone star belt buckles and old faded Levi's
And each night begins a new day
If you don't understand him and he don't die young
He'll probably just ride away

Mamas, don't let your babies grow up to be cowboys
Don't let 'em pick guitars and drive them old trucks
Let 'em be doctors and lawyers and such
Mamas, don't let your babies grow up to be cowboys
They'll never stay home and they're always alone
Even with someone they love

Russell and Remington
"Cowboy Artists"

Anonymous

Imagine you own a time machine and you choose to travel back in history to the old American West . . . specifically to the wild Montana Territory of the 1860s and 70s. What you might be lucky to observe is two renowned cowboy artists, Frederick Remington and Charles Russell.

Imagine coming upon them sketching—with charcoal and/or color sticks—the great Western experience. Perhaps Indian braves hunting buffalo, or the U.S. cavalry giving homesteaders safe passage, or cowboys breaking broncos for range riding. From these scenes Russell and Remington sketched, painted, and sculpted great pieces of art—capturing the action and romance of the old West.

Desperado

By Don Henley and Glenn Frey

Desperado, why don't you come to your senses?
You been out riding fences for so long now
Oh you're a hard one, but I know that you've got your reasons
Those things that are pleasin' you will hurt you somehow

Don't you draw the queen of diamonds, boy
She'll beat you if she's able
You know the queen of hearts is always your best bet
Now it seems to me some fine things
Have been laid upon your table
But you only want the ones that you can't get

Desperado, you know you ain't gettin' younger
Your pain and your hunger they're driving you home
And freedom, oh freedom, that's just some people talkin'
Your prison is walking through this world all alone

Don't your feet get cold in the wintertime
The sky won't snow and the sun won't shine
It's hard to tell the nighttime from the day
You're losing all your highs and lows
Ain't it funny how the feeling goes away

Come down from your fences, open the gate
It may be rainin', but there's a rainbow above you
You better let somebody love you—before it's too late

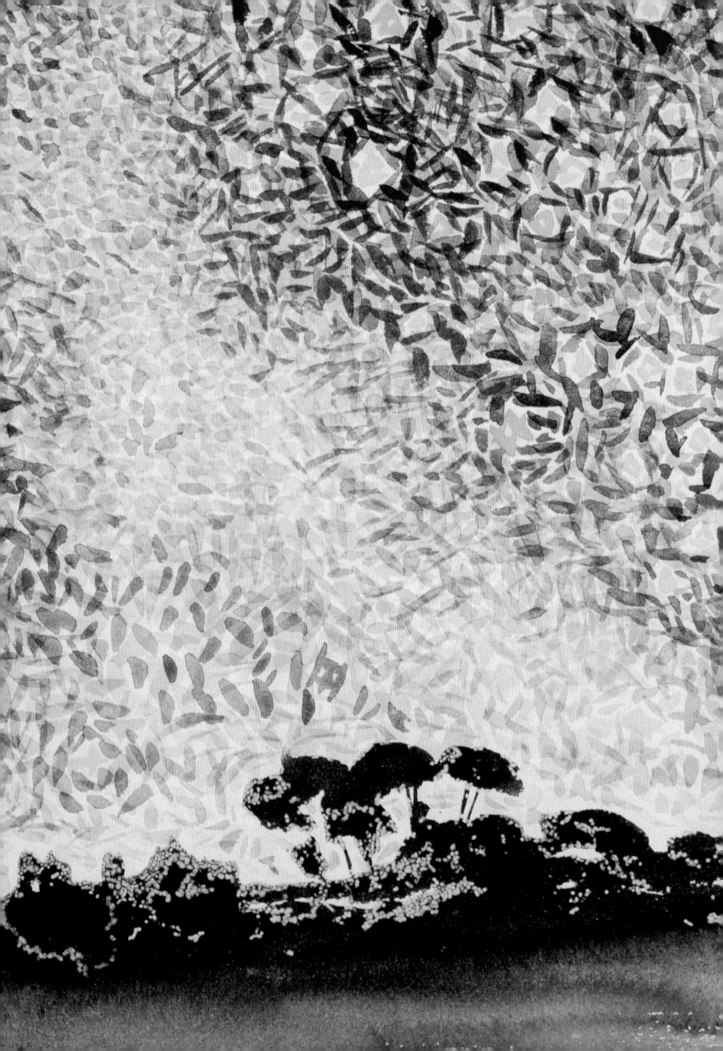

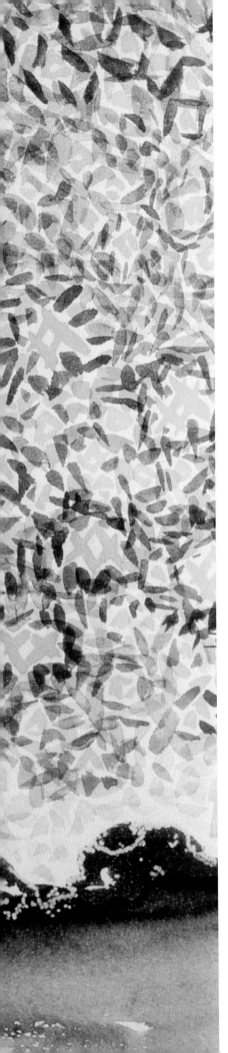

Deep in the Heart of Texas

By June Hershey and Don Swander

The stars at night are big and bright
[clap, clap, clap, clap]
Deep in the heart of Texas.

The prairie sky is wide and high
[clap, clap, clap, clap]
Deep in the heart of Texas.

The sage in bloom is like perfume
[clap, clap, clap, clap]
Deep in the heart of Texas.

Reminds me of the one I love
[clap, clap, clap, clap]
Deep in the heart of Texas.

The coyotes wail along the trail
[clap, clap, clap, clap]
Deep in the heart of Texas.

The rabbits rush around the brush
[clap, clap, clap, clap]
Deep in the heart of Texas.

The cowboys cry "Ki-yip-pee-yi"
[clap, clap, clap, clap]
Deep in the heart of Texas.

The dogies bawl and bawl and bawl
[clap, clap, clap, clap]
Deep in the heart of Texas.

The Child Is Introduced to the Cosmos at Birth

Anonymous Omaha song

Ho! Ye Sun, Moon, Stars,
    all ye that move in the heavens,
    I bid you hear me!
Into your midst has come a new life.
    Consent ye, I implore!
Make its path smooth, that it may reach
    The brow of the first hill!

Ho! Ye Winds, Clouds, Rain, Mist,
    all ye that move in the air,
    I bid you hear me!
Into your midst has come a new life.
    Consent ye, I implore!
Make its path smooth, that it may reach
    The brow of the second hill!

Ho! Ye Hills, Valleys, River, Lakes, Trees, Grasses,
    all ye of the earth,
    I bid you hear me!
Into your midst has come a new life.
    Consent ye, I implore!
Make its path smooth, that it may reach
    The brow of the third hill!

Ho! Ye Birds, great and small, that fly in the air,
Ho! Ye Animals, great and small, that dwell in the forest,
Ho! Ye Insects that creep among the grasses and burrow in the ground:
    I bid you hear me!
Into your midst has come a new life.
    Consent ye, I implore!
Make its path smooth, that it may reach
    The brow of the fourth hill!

Ho! All ye of the heavens, all ye of the air, all ye of the earth:
    I bid you all to hear me!
Into your midst has come a new life.
    Consent ye, consent ye all, I implore!
Make its path smooth—then shall it travel
    Beyond the four hills.

Sweet Betsy from Pike

An excerpt

Anonymous

Oh, don't you remember Sweet Betsy from Pike?
Who crossed the big mountains with her lover Ike.
With two yoke of Oxen, a big yaller dog,
A tall Shanghai rooster, and one spotted hog.
Hoodle dang folde dido hoodle dang folde day.

One evening quite early they camped on the Platte.
'Twas nearby the road on a green shady flat
Where Betsy, sore-footed, lay down to repose.
With wonder Ike gazed on his Pike County rose.
Hoodle dang folde dido hoodle dang folde day.

The Shanghai ran off, and their cattle all died,
That morning the last piece of bacon was fried.
Poor Ike was discouraged and Betsy got mad.
The dog dropped his tail and looked wondrously sad.
Hoodle dang folde dido hoodle dang folde day.

They soon reached the desert where Betsy gave out.
And down in the sand she lay rolling about,
While Ike half distracted looked on with surprise,
Saying, "Betsy, get up, you'll get sand in your eyes."
Hoodle dang folde dido hoodle dang folde day.

Sweet Betsy got up in a great deal of pain,
Declared she'd go back to Pike County again.
But Ike gave a sigh, and they fondly embraced,
And they traveled along with his arm 'round her waist.
Hoodle dang folde dido hoodle dang folde day.

What the Engines Said

*The joining of the Union Pacific and
Central Pacific Railroads, May 10, 1869*

By Brett Harte

What was it the Engines said,
Pilots touching, head to head,
Facing on the single track,
Half a world behind each back?
This is what the Engines said,
Unreported and unread.

With a prefatory screech,
In a florid Western speech,
Said the Engine from the West:
"I am from Sierra's crest;
And if altitude's a test,
Why, I reckon, it's confessed
That I've done my level best."

Said the Engine from the East:
"They who work best talk the least.
S'pose you whistle down your brakes;
What you've done is no great shakes,
Pretty fair, but let our meeting
Be a different kind of greeting.
Let these folks with champagne stuffing,
Not their Engines, do the puffing.

"Listen! Where Atlantic beats
Shores of snow and summer heats;
Where the Indian autumn skies
Paint the woods with wampum dyes,
I have chased the flying sun,
Seeing all he looked upon,
Blessing all that he has blessed,
Nursing in my iron breast
All his vivifying heat,

All his clouds about my crest;
And before my flying feet
Every shadow must retreat."

Said the Western Engine: "Phew!"
And a long, low whistle blew.
"Come, now, really that's the oddest
Talk for one so very modest.
You brag of your East! You do?
Why, I bring the East to you!
All the Orient, all Cathay,
Find through me the shortest way;
And the sun you follow here
Rises in my hemisphere.
Really, if one must be rude,
Length, my friend, ain't longitude."

Said the Union: "Don't reflect, or
I'll run over some Director."
Said the Central: "I'm Pacific;
But, when riled, I'm quite terrific.
Yet today we shall not quarrel,
Just to show these folks this moral,
How two Engines—in their vision—
Once have met without collision."

This is what the Engines said,
Unreported and unread:
Spoken slightly through the nose,
With a whistle at the close.

Ogalalla: Indian Love Song

By Vincent Bryan

Ogalalla, Ogalalla,
At the end of all things,
My love, we will say again,
We never loved, we never lived
Anywhere, but in heaven.

Ogalalla, Ogalalla,
At the end of our dream
My love, we will believe,
We never loved, we never lived
But in a continuous dream.

Paul Bunyan and His Great Blue Ox

An excerpt

By Wallace Wadsworth

The Great Blue Ox was so strong that he could pull anything that had two ends and some things that had no ends at all, which made him very valuable at times, as one can easily understand.

Babe was remarkable in a number of ways besides that of his color, which was a bright blue. His size is rather a matter of doubt, some people holding that he was twenty-four ax handles and a plug of tobacco wide between the eyes, and others saying that he was forty-two ax handles across the forehead. It may be that both

are wrong, for the story goes that Jim, the pet crow, who always roosted on Babe's left horn, one day decided to fly across to the tip of the other horn. He got lost on the way and didn't get to the other horn until after the spring thaw, and he had started in the dead of winter.

The Great Blue Ox was so long in the body that an ordinary person, standing at his head, would have had to use a pair of field glasses in order to see what the animal was doing with his hind feet.

Babe had a great love for Paul and a peculiar way of showing it, which discovered the great logger's only weakness. Paul was ticklish, especially around the neck, and the Ox had a strong passion for licking him there with his tongue. His master good-naturedly avoided such outbursts of affection from his pet whenever possible.

One day Paul took the Blue Ox with him to town, and there he loaded him with all the supplies that would be needed for the camp and crew during the winter. When everything had been packed on Babe's back, the animal was so heavily laden that on the way back to camp he sank to his knees in the solid rock at nearly every step. These footprints later filled with water and became the countless lakes that are to be found today scattered throughout the state of Maine.

Babe was compelled to go slowly, of course, on account of the great load he carried, and so Paul had to camp overnight along the way. He took the packs from the Ox's back, turned the big animal out to graze, and after eating supper he lay down to sleep.

The Blue Ox, however, was for some strange reason in a restless mood that night, and after feeding all that he cared to, he wandered away for many miles before he finally found a

place that suited his particular idea of what a bedding ground should be. There he lay down, and it is quite possible that he was very much amused in thinking of the trouble which his master would have in finding him the next morning. The Ox was a very wise creature, and every now and then he liked to play a little joke on Paul.

Along about dawn Paul Bunyan awoke and looked about for his pet. Not a glimpse of him could he get in any direction, though he whistled so loudly for him that the nearby trees were shattered into bits. At last, after he had eaten his breakfast, and Babe still did not appear, Paul knew that the joke was on him. "He thinks he has put up a little trick on me," he said to himself with a grin. Paul set off trailing the missing animal.

Babe's tracks were so large that it took three men, standing close together, to see across one of them, and they were so far apart that no one could follow them but Paul, who was an expert trailer, no one else ever being able to equal him in this ability. So remarkable was he in this respect that he could follow any tracks that were ever made, no matter how old or how faint they were. It is told of him that he once came across the carcass of a bull moose that had died of old age, and having a couple of hours to spare, and being also of an inquiring turn of mind, he followed the tracks of the moose back to the place where it had been born.

Being such an expert, therefore, it did not take him very long to locate Babe. The Great Blue Ox, when he at last came across him, was lying down contentedly chewing his cud and waiting for his master to come and find him. "You worthless critter!" Paul said to him, and thwacked him good-naturedly with his hand. "Look at the trouble you have put me to, and just look at the damage you have done here," and he pointed to the great hollow place in the ground that Babe had wallowed out while lying there. The Ox's only reply was to smother Paul for a moment with a loving, juicy lick of his great tongue.

Anyone, by looking at a map of the state of Maine, can easily locate Moosehead Lake, which is, as history shows, the place where the Great Blue Ox lay down.

No one, certainly, could be expected to copy him in the matter of straightening out crooked logging trails. It was all wild country where Paul did his logging, and about the only roads that he found through the woods were the trails and paths made by the wild animals that had traveled over them for hundreds of years. Paul decided to use these game trails as logging roads, but they twisted and turned in every direction and were all so crooked that they had to be straightened before any use could be made of them. It is well known that the Great Blue Ox was so powerful that he could pull anything that had two ends, and so when Paul wanted a crooked logging trail straightened out, he would just hitch Babe up to one end of it, tell his pet to go ahead, and, lo and behold, the crooked trail would be pulled out perfectly straight!

There was one particularly bad stretch of road, about twenty or thirty miles long, that gave Babe and Paul a lot of trouble before they finally got all the crooks pulled out of it. It certainly must have been the crookedest road in the world—it twisted and turned so much that it spelled out every letter of the alphabet, some of the letters two or three times. Paul taught Babe how to read just by leading him over it a few times, and men going along it met themselves coming from the other direction so often that the whole camp was near crazy before long.

So Paul decided that the road would have to be straightened out without any further delay, and with that end in view he ordered a chain made which had links four feet long and two feet across, and the steel they were made of was thirteen inches thick.

The chain being ready, Paul hitched Babe up to one end of the road with it. At his master's word, the Great Blue Ox began to puff and pull and strain away as he had never done before, and at last he got the end pulled out a little ways. Paul chirped to him again, and he pulled away harder then ever. With every tug he made, one of the twists in the road would straighten out, and then Babe would pull away again, hind legs straight out behind and belly to the ground. It was the hardest job Babe had ever been put up against, but he stuck to it admirably.

When the task was finally done the Ox was nearly fagged out, a condition that he had never known before, and that big chain had been pulled on so hard that it was pulled out into a solid steel bar. The road was straightened out, however, which was the thing Paul wanted, and he considered the time and energy expended as well worthwhile, since the nuisance had been transformed into something useful. He found, though, that since all the kinks and twists had been pulled out, there was now a whole lot more of the road than was needed, but—never being a person who could stand to waste anything that might be useful—he rolled up all the extra length and laid it down in a place where there had never been a road before but where one might come in handy sometime.

Nor was the straightening of crooked roads the only useful work which the Great Blue Ox did. It was also his task to skid or drag the logs from the stumps to rollways by the streams, where they were stored for the drives. Babe was always obedient, and a tireless and patient worker. It is said that the timber of nineteen states, except a few scant sections here and there that Paul Bunyan did not touch, was skidded from the stumps by the all-powerful Great Blue Ox. He was docile and willing, and could be depended upon for the performance of almost any task set him, except that once in a while he would develop a sudden streak of mischief and drink a river dry behind a drive or run off into the woods. Sometimes he would step on a ridge that formed the bank of the river and smash it down so that the river would start running out through his tracks, thus changing its course entirely from what Paul had counted on.

Happy Trails

By Dale Evans

Some trails are happy ones,
Others are blue.
It's the way you ride the trail that counts;
Here's a happy one for you:

Happy trails to you until we meet again
Happy trails to you, keep smilin' until then.

Who cares about the clouds when we're together?
Just sing a song and bring the sunny weather.

Happy trails to you until we meet again
Happy trails to you, keep smilin' until then.

This Land Is Your Land

An excerpt

By Woody Guthrie

This land is your land, this land is my land,
From California to the New York Island,
From the redwood forest to the Gulf Stream waters—
This land was made for you and me.

As I went walking that ribbon of highway
I saw above me that endless skyway,
I saw below me that golden valley—
This land was made for you and me.

As I went walking I saw a sign there
And on the sign it said, "No Tresspassing,"
But on the other side it didn't say nothing—
That side was made for you and me.

Nobody living can ever stop me
As I go walking my freedom highway.
Nobody living can ever make me turn back—
This land was made for you and me.

This land is your land, this land is my land,
From California to the New York Island,
From the redwood forest to the gulf stream waters—
This land was made for you and me.

Don't Fence Me In

By Cole Porter

Oh, give me land, lots of land under starry skies above,
Don't fence me in.
Let me ride through the wide open country that I love,
Don't fence me in.

Let me be by myself in the evening breeze,
Listen to the murmur of the cottonwood trees.
Send me off forever, but I ask you please,
Don't fence me in; just turn me loose.

Let me straddle my old saddle underneath the western skies.
On my cayuse, let me wander over yonder till I see the mountains rise.
I want to ride to the ridge where the West commences,
Gaze at the moon till I lose my senses,
Can't look at hobbles and I can't stand fences,
Don't fence me in.

The Sheaves

By Edwin Arlington Robinson

Where long the shadows of the wind had rolled,
Green wheat was yielding to the change assigned;
And as by some vast magic undivined
The world was turning slowly into gold.
Like nothing that was ever bought or sold
It waited there, the body and the mind;
And with a mighty meaning of a kind
That tells the more the more it is not told.

So in a land where all days are not fair,
Fair days went on till on another day
A thousand golden sheaves were lying there,
Shining and still, but not for long to stay—
As if a thousand girls with golden hair
Might rise from where they slept and go away.

The Prince of the Pistoleers

Anonymous dime-novel advertisement

After his days as a cavalry scout and marshal in Dodge City,
With his long and graceful mourning jacket and his broad-brimmed black hat,
You might even say Ol' Wild Bill was a dandy—poised, polished, and pretty.

While Ol' Wild Bill patrolled Deadwood
Gunfighters trembled with many tears and fears
Such was the prowess of Wild Bill Hickok in his legendary years
Known by every gunman who faced him as The Prince of the Pistoleers.

Ol' Wild Bill's aim with his dual Colt 45s could not be denied,
Before his target's heart Bill made two gold bullets harmlessly collide
Such was the prowess of Wild Bill Hickok in his legendary years
Known by every gunman who faced him as The Prince of the Pistoleers.

My Sweet Wyoming Home

An excerpt

By Bill Staines

There's a silence on the prairie that a man can't help but feel
There's a shadow growing longer now, a-nipping at my heels
I know that soon that old four-lane that runs beneath my wheels
Will take me home . . .
to my sweet Wyoming home

I headed down the road last summer with a few old friends of mine
They all hit the money, Lord, I didn't make a dime
The entrance fees they took my dough, the traveling took my time
And I'm headed home . . .
to my sweet Wyoming home

Watch the moon, it's smiling in the sky
And hum a tune, a prairie lullaby
Peaceful wind and old coyote's cry
A song of home . . .
my sweet Wyoming home

The rounders they all wish you luck
when they know you're in a jam
But your money's riding on the bull
and he don't give a damn
The songs I'm used to hearing ain't the
kind the jukebox slam
And I'm headed home . . .
to my sweet Wyoming home

And now I've always loved the riding,
there ain't nothing quite the same
And another year may bring the luck,
the winning of the game
But there's a magpie on a fence rail and
he's calling out my name
And he calls me home . . .
to my sweet Wyoming home

Little Chipmunks and Great Owls

An excerpt from The Power of Myth

By Joseph Campbell

It's a different kind of world to grow up in when you're out in the forest with little chipmunks and the great owls. All these things are around you as presences, representing forces and powers and magic possibilities of life that are all part of living, and all opening out to you. Then you find it echoing in yourself, because you are nature and you are enjoying that refreshment, that life within you, all the time.

The Brave Man

By Wallace Stevens

The sun, that brave man,
Comes through boughs that lie in wait,
That brave man.

Green and gloomy eyes
In dark forms of grass
Run away.

The good stars,
Pale helms and spiky spurs,
Run away.

Fears of my bed,
Fears of life and fears of death,
Run away.

That brave man comes up
From below and walks without meditation,
That brave man.

Buffalo Bill's Wild West Show

By Charles P. Graves

One of the most famous buffalo hunters and Indian fighters in America was a man named William S. Cody. He was called "Buffalo Bill." When he stopped fighting Indians, he started a Wild West Show. He wanted people in the eastern part of America to see what the West was really like. The people who came to his show saw wild buffalo, deer, elk, and bear. They saw Indians wearing war bonnets, the feathers trailing to the ground. The show had cowboys who rode bucking horses, who wrangled calves to the ground with lariats or wrastled steers off their feet with their strong arms. There were make-believe bandits who robbed a stagecoach and a pretend battle between the cavalry and many Indian warriors. The show also featured good shooters.

Everybody liked Annie Oakley's act. She rode into the arena on a snow-white horse. Annie wore a buckskin skirt and shirt. Her chestnut hair flashed below her cowboy hat. Her blue eyes shone with excitement. Frank Butler threw some glass balls into the air. Annie, still on horseback, raised her gun. "Crack!" With each shot Annie broke a glass ball. Then Annie got off her horse. Frank held a coin between his thumb and forefinger. Annie shot the coin out of his fingers. Next he held up a playing card. Annie shot the spots out of it. A wheel with lighted candles started to spin. Annie shot the flames and put the candles out.

The Lone Ranger and Tonto

Television show opening monologue

A fiery horse with the speed of light, a cloud of dust, and a hearty "Hi-yo Silver!" The Lone Ranger! With his faithful Indian companion, Tonto, the daring and resourceful masked rider of the plains led the fight for law and order in the early West. Return with us now to those thrilling days of yesteryear—the Lone Ranger rides again!

Thank You, Masked Man—
Thank You, Clayton Moore

By Sam Donato

In the 1960s I worked as an actor at Pleasure Island Amusement Park in Wakefield, Massachusetts. It was a great job for the young at heart, because our duties required us to emcee stage shows and play Cowboys and Indians for the benefit of the people who came to the park. We also had to assist the many celebrities who came to make personal appearances.

One day the park announcer and I were called into the office of the general manager to be briefed on the requirements of our next celebrity—Clayton Moore. Clayton Moore! The Lone Ranger!

We were then told that he would be arriving in two days and preparations had to be made. Wow! We were thrilled! We went to work to make his stay as pleasant as possible. Finally the day came for Mr. Moore's arrival.

"Hello, gentlemen. My name is Clayton Moore," he said upon our first meeting. His voice may as well have been a thunderclap for the way it struck me. That was the Voice, the voice of the Lone Ranger.

He then gave us a rough format of what he was to do for the show. He would ride into the show bowl from the top of the hill on Silver. He would then do some tricks, dismount, and come up on the stage to talk to the crowd.

The next day the first show was scheduled at 2:00 PM. It was standing room only as parents and kids crowded into the bowl not quite sure what they were going to see. As the general welcome and introduction continued I scanned the hill waiting for the cue; then I heard it. The resounding William Tell Overture.

The park announcer started the famous introduction. I was enthralled. Then just as the announcer got to the words, "Return with us now to those thrilling days of yesteryear—the Lone Ranger rides again," I looked to the hill again and there he was!

The crowd gasped! They had good reason to. There on the hill astride his horse, Silver, was a man who looked ten feet tall. He reared Silver up, and his front hoofs pawed the air. The exhilaration charged the crowd.

From that point on, the show went just as he had planned it. Clayton Moore spoke of the high ideals the Ranger stood for and how in all the films, the Ranger never killed anyone. The audience listened and believed. They really believed he was the Lone Ranger. And I believed. I believed this man, Clayton Moore, took his responsibility to his young fans absolutely seriously. His smile, his warmth, and his voice couldn't be a put-on.

The Cowboy's Lament

Anonymous

As I walked out on the streets of Laredo
As I walked out in Laredo one day
I spied a poor cowboy wrapped in white linen
Wrapped up in white linen as cold as clay

"I see by your outfit that you are a cowboy"
These words he did say as I boldly stepped by
"Come sit down beside me and hear my sad story
I am shot in the breast and I know I must die

"My friends and relations they live in the Nation
They know not where their boy has gone
I first came to Texas and hired to a ranchman
Oh, I'm a young cowboy and I know I've done wrong

"It was once in the saddle I used to go dashing
It was once in the saddle I used to go gay
First to the dram house and then to the card house
Got shot in the breast and I am dying today

"Get six jolly cowboys to carry my coffin
Get six pretty maidens to bear up my pall
Put bunches of roses all over my coffin
Roses to deaden the clods as they fall

"Oh beat the drum slowly and play the fife lowly
Play the Dead March as you carry me on
Take me out to the graveyard and throw sod o'er me
For I'm a young cowboy and I know I've done wrong

"Go gather around you a group of young cowboys
And tell them the story of this my sad fate
Tell one and the other before they go further
To stop their wild roving before it's too late

"Go bring me a cup, a cup of cold water
To cool my parched lips," the cowboy then said
But 'ere I returned the spirit had left him
And gone to its maker: the cowboy was dead

We beat the drum slowly and played the fife lowly
And bitterly wept as we bore him along
For we all loved our comrade so brave, young, and handsome
We all loved the cowboy altho' he'd done wrong

Red Wing: An Indian Fable

By Thurland Chattaway

There once lived an Indian maid,
A shy little prairie maid,
Who sang a lay, a love song gay,
As on the plain she'd while away the day.

She loved a warrior bold,
This shy little maid of old,
But brave and gay he rode one day
To battle far away.

Now the moon shines tonight on pretty Red Wing
The breeze is sighing, the night bird's crying.
For far beneath his star her brave is sleeping,
While Red Wing's weeping her heart away.

She watched for him day and night,
She kept all the campfires bright,
And under the sky, each night she would lie,
And dream about his coming by and by.

But when all the braves returned,
The heart of Red Wing yearned
For far, far away, her warrior gay
Fell bravely in the fray.

Now the moon shines tonight on pretty Red Wing
The breeze is sighing, the night bird's crying.
For far beneath his star her brave is sleeping,
While Red Wing's weeping her heart away.

Git Along Little Dogies

An excerpt

Anonymous

As I walked out one morning for pleasure,
I spied a cowpuncher a-ridin' alone;
His hat was throwed back and his spurs were a-jinglin'
As he approached me a-singin' this song:

Whoopee ti yi yo, git along little dogies.
It's your misfortune and none of my own.
Whoopie to yi yo, git along little dogies.
For you know Wyoming will be your new home.

Early in the spring we round up the dogies,
Mark 'em and brand 'em and bob off their tails;
Round up our horses, load up the chuckwagon,
Then throw the dogies upon the old trail.

It's whooping and yelling and driving the dogies;
Oh, how I wish you would go on!
It's whooping and punching and "Go on little dogies,"
For you know Wyoming will be your new home.

Whoopee ti yi yo, git along little dogies.
It's your misfortune and none of my own.
Whoopie to yi yo, git along little dogies.
For you know Wyoming will be your new home.

Gunfight at the O.K. Corral

By Cathy Luchetti

Violence could erupt from either side of the law. No tin star could shine up a reprobate lawman. Marshals and sheriffs, masters of their territories, were often lawless themselves and quick judges of who should stay and who should go.

Wyatt Earp was another to move between law and outlaw. Elected constable of Lamar, Missouri, in 1870, he was a conscientious lawman until his wife died of typhoid two years later. Earp drifted into Indian Territory and was soon arrested for stealing horses. In 1874 he joined his brother James in Wichita, Kansas, and worked as a policeman, again proving to be reliable and conscientious. Later he worked first as a policeman, then as an assistant marshal of Dodge City, where he struck up friendships with gamblers Doc Holliday and Bat Masterson. Earp joined his four brothers in Tombstone, Arizona, where brother Virgil was temporary town marshal, was replaced, and then become permanent town marshal after his replacement mysteriously disappeared. Virgil and Wyatt invited their gambling friends Holliday and Masterson to join them. As lawmen they ruled until opposed by a coalition of small ranchers led by the Clanton family.

In 1881, the feud with the Clanton gang ended with the famous Gunfight at the O.K. Corral. Three of the Clanton gang were killed. The three Earp brothers—Virgil, Wyatt, and Morgan—survived, along with Doc Holliday.

After the shoot-out their affairs declined, even though the Earps were vindicated as acting within the law. Revenge, threats, gunplay, and killings followed the brothers. Wyatt gambled professionally in the mining camps of Nevada and Arizona, and his brother Virgil finally joined him, opening a gambling hall in San Diego in the 1890s. Their behavior veered back and forth between legality and criminality.

The Shooting of Dan McGrew

By Robert Service

A bunch of the boys were whooping it up in the Malamute saloon;
The kid that handles the music-box was hitting a jag-time tune;
Back at the bar, in a solo game, sat Dangerous Dan McGrew,
And watching his luck was his light-o'-love, the lady that's known as Lou.

When out of the night, which was fifty below, and into the din and the glare,
There stumbled a miner fresh from the creeks, dog-dirty and loaded for bear.
He looked like a man with a foot in the grave and scarcely the strength of a louse,
Yet he tilted a poke of dust on the bar, and he called for drinks for the house.
There was none could place the stranger's face, though we searched ourselves for a clue;
But we drank his health; and the last to drink was Dangerous Dan McGrew.

There's men that somehow just grip your eyes, and hold them hard like a spell;
And such was he, and he looked to me like a man who had lived in hell;
With a face most hair, and the dreary stare of a dog whose day is done,
He watered the green stuff in his glass, and the drops fell one by one.
Then I got to figgering who he was, and wondering what he'd do,
And I turned my head—and there watching him was the lady that's known as Lou.

His eyes went rubbering round the room, and he seemed in a kind of daze,
Till at last that old piano fell in the way of his wandering gaze.
The ragtime kid was having a drink; there was no one else on the stool,
So the stranger stumbles across the room, and flops down there like a fool.
In a buckskin shirt that was glazed with dirt he sat, and I saw him sway;
Then he clutched the keys with his talon hands—my God, but that man could play!

Were you ever out in the Great Alone, when the moon was awful clear,
And the icy mountains hemmed you in with a silence you most could *hear*;
With only the howl of a timber wolf, and you camped there in the cold,
A half-dead thing in a stark, dead world, clean mad for the muck called gold;
While high overhead, green, yellow and red, the North Lights swept in bars?—
Then you've a hunch what the music meant . . . hunger and night and the stars.

And hunger not of the belly kind that's banished with bacon and beans,
But the gnawing hunger of lonely men for a home and all that it means;
For a fireside far from the cares that are, four walls and a roof above;

But oh! So cramful of cozy joy, and crowned with a woman's love—
A woman dearer than all the world, and true as Heaven is true . . .
(God! how ghastly she looks through her rouge—the lady that's known as Lou.)

Then on a sudden the music changed, so soft that you scarce could hear;
But you felt that your life had been looted clean of all that it once held dear;
That someone had stolen the woman you loved; that her love was a devil's lie;
That your guts were gone, and the best for you was to crawl away and die.
'Twas the crowning cry of a heart's despair, and it thrilled you through and through—
"I guess I'll make it a spread misère," said Dangerous Dan McGrew.

The music almost died away . . . then it burst like a pent-up flood;
And it seemed to say, "Repay, repay," and my eyes were blind with blood.
The thought came back of an ancient wrong, and it stung like a frozen lash,
And the lust awoke to kill, to kill . . . then the music stopped with a crash,
And the stranger turned, and his eyes they burned in a most peculiar way;
In a buckskin shirt that was glazed with dirt he sat, and I saw him sway;
Then his lips went in in a kind of grin, and he spoke, and his voice was calm,
And "Boys," says he, "you don't know me, and none of you care a damn;
But I want to state, and my words are straight, and I'll bet my poke they're true,
That one of you is a hound of hell . . . and that one is Dan McGrew."

Then I ducked my head, and the lights went out, and two guns blazed in the dark,
And a woman screamed, and the lights went up, and the two men lay stiff and stark.
Pitched on his head, and pumped full of lead, was Dangerous Dan McGrew,
While the man from the creeks lay clutched to the breast of the lady that's known as Lou.

These are the simple facts of the case, and I guess I ought to know.
They say that the stranger was crazed with "hooch" and I'm not denying it's so.
I'm not so wise as the lawyer guys, but strictly between us two—
The woman that kissed him—and pinched his poke—was the lady that's known as Lou.

America the Beautiful

An excerpt

By Katharine Lee Bates and Samuel A. Ward

O beautiful for spacious skies,
For amber waves of grain,
For purple mountain majesties
Above the fruited plain!
America! America!
God shed His grace on thee,
And crown thy good with brotherhood
From sea to shining sea!

The Five Stork Birth

An excerpt from Paul Bunyan and Resinous Rhymes of the North Woods

By Thomas G. Alvord Jr.

Big Michael O'Leary—we called him "the Squirrel"
    On account of his bein' so agile—
And Glass Eye McBride—whom we dubbed "Glass" for short,
    Him bein' in parts rather fragile—
Was arguin' some about big "cuts" and such,
    The drive years before on the Onion,
And the talk got around where we all spun a yarn,
    And had somethin' to say about Bunyan.
Says I to the Squirrel—it was him I addressed,
    For it seemed that he'd given some study
To matters pertainin' to Bunyan's career,
    And I figured, although rather muddy,
His knowledge perhaps, since his grandpap O'Shane
    As a young feller knew Bunyan well,
Might enable him some, if he'd be so inclined,
    To review what he knew, and to tell
Both the tales he'd heard through his grandpappy's talk,
    And the ones, which he'd gathered in camps,
The sum of the twain such as might make a book,
    Or a pen-pusher ill with the cramps.
As I say, I spoke up and addressed my old friend,
    And I says to him: "Squirrel, do you know
As regards to the birth of this Paul Bunyan chap,
    Of his kin, of his parents? If so,
I'd certainly like to get straight to my mind
    Some facts upon which to depend,
For all that I've heard are conflictin' reports,
    Which leads me, of course, to contend
That Paul was a fake; but a fantastic dream
    his feats which, it's claimed, he performed."
"But it's just as I say, there's no good reason to think
    That I've been a lot misinformed.
'Twas a night some like this," so continues Squirrel,
    As he peers through the spruce at the moon,
"Which is risin' up full off across the muskeg,

Like a mammoth inflated balloon,
When a feller named Hodgins—a native back Maine—
 A bit over-loaded and weary,
Comes weavin' along with his jug and his jag,
 A-eyein' the tote-road some bleary.
He's singin' a song, which he chants mou'nful-like,
 Regardin' his Slaughterhouse Lily;
A right mou'nful tune, but it seems that it suits
 His mood on this drunken occasion,
For he's rounded it off for the fifty-sixth time
 When he sees him a sight that's hair-raisin'
Loomin' up 'fore his eyes, 'twixt the swamp and the moon,
 And this Hodgins comes near to chokin'
For the strange things he sees, high over the trees,
 Is a passel o' five storks a-flappin',
And 'twixt them a blanket, in chick there's a child,
 Unusually boisterous and strappin'.
But he notes while he gapes, with his eyes bulgin' big,
 That the storks are a-fixin' to light,
So hidin' himself in the brush close at hand,
 Where he's certain to be out o' sight,

He watches and waits, and it won't be very long
    Till sure enough, down all kerthud,
Them storks and their freight comes a-bustin' through space,
    And lands in a heap in the mud.
Well them natal birds, with their wings about broke,
    And exhausted from strenuous flight,
Of course are ashamed a great deal by the fact
    That they've fallen some short of the site
Where the Bunyans abide in the big timber near,
    And in council decide that they'll try
By effort supreme and by will most superb
    To continue their journey, or die.
But this infant—this lad—who, you must know, was Paul,
    From his blanket kicks loose in a hurry,
And stands up erect and addresses his crew,
    And, says he, 'My good fellows, don't worry.
I'm able, indeed, and I wish to proceed,
    But a stranger I am in this section,
So give me a guide to walk by my side,
    To show me the proper direction.'
Quite unusual, unique, and, I might say, sublime,
    Was the conduct of Paul this particular time,
For upon his arrival at Bunyan's abode,
    He said naught to his ma, but deliberately strode
To the pantry where victuals piled high on the shelf,
    Permitted his gettin' a meal for his-self."

Song of Myself

An excerpt

By Walt Whitman

A gigantic beauty of a stallion, fresh and responsive to my caresses.
Head high in the forehead, wide between the ears,
Limbs glossy and supple, tail dusting the ground,
Eyes full of sparkling wickedness, ears finely cut, flexibly moving.
His nostrils dilate as my heels embrace him,
His well-built limbs tremble with pleasure as we race around and return.

Schoolcraft's Diary, Written on the Missouri, 1830

By Robert Bly

Waters are loose: from Judith and the Larb,
Straining and full, the thick Missouri, choked
With sticks and roots, and high with floating trees
And spoils of snowfields from the Crazy Hills,
Burns loose earth off. The brown Missouri's mouth
Eats earth a hundred feet below the plains.
At dawn we see the crumbling cliffs at first,
Then horse and rider, then the eastern sky.
At daybreak riders shout from western cliffs.
The buffalo, in herds, come down to drink.
Turn back, and shoulders humping, racket on
Up dust-chewn paths onto the plains of dust;
And I have heard the buffalo stampede
With muffled clatter of colliding horns.
A subtle peril hangs above this land
Like smoke that floats at dawn above dead fires.

The dead in scaffolds float on steady rafts,
Corroding in their sepulchers of air.
At dawn the Osage part their tepee doors,
Cutting their arms and thighs with sharp-edged shells.
The dark-blue buzzard flocks awake on trees
And stretch their black wings toward the sun to dry.
Such are few details that I have seen.

And there are signs of what will come: the whites
With steel traps hanging, swung from saddle thongs.
The busy whites believe these Sioux and Kaws
And Mandans are not men at all, but beasts:
Some snake-bound beast, regressed, embedded, wound,
Held in damnation, and by death alone
To be released. The Sioux are still and silent
Generally, and I have watched them stand
By ones and twos upon the riverbank,
As still as Hudson's blankets winding them.

While shuttling steamboats, smoking, labor up,
Invading the landscape of their youth and dreams,
Pushed up, they say, by smoke; and they believe
This tribe of whites, like smoke, soon shall return
From where it came. The truth drops out of mind,
As if the pain of action were so great
And life so freezing and Medusa-faced
That, like Medusa's head, it could be held
And not observed, lest its reward be stone.
Now night grows old above this riverboat.
Before I end, I shall include account
Of an incident tonight that moved my wonder.
At dusk we tied the ship to trees on shore;
No mortal boat in these night shoals can live.
At first I heard a cry, then shufflings, steps.
The muffled sounds on deck oak overhead
Drew me on deck. The air was chill, and there
I sensed, because these senses here are sharp
And must be, something living and unknown.
To night and north a crowd stared from the boatrail,
Upriver, northward, nightward; a speck of white.
The thing was white: the resonance of night
Returned its whiffs and whistlings on the air.
The frontiermen swore in that river thicket,
In ambush like the lizards they're modeled on,
Bristling for war, would be a thresh of Sioux.
But Mormons see some robe in that faint white,
An angel of death upon the chill Missouri.
One man believed that there was nothing there,
As the moon is false, and all its light is false.
I felt a fear, as if it were protected.
When the talk died, eight men, and I with them,
Set off and, moving overboard in dark,
With guns, protected by the thunder's noise,
Up the dark stream, toward where the splashes rose,
So armed in case of Sioux, to our surprise
We found a white and wounded northern bear,
Shot in that day about the snout and head.

The pure-white bear, not native to these parts,
But to the Horns, or Ranges, born, and shot
That morning had turned west or south in pain.
Turned west, to lay its burning paws and head
Within the cool Missouri's turbid bed.
I felt as I had once when through a door,
At ten or twelve, I'd seen my mother bathing.
Soon after, clouds of rain fell in sheets; such rain
Said to be sudden in these Western lands.
Minutes before it broke, a circling mass
Of split-tail swallows came and then were gone.

Battle of the Little Big Horn

An excerpt

Anonymous survivor's description

We arrived on the bank of the Little Bighorn River and waded to the other side. Here the water was about three feet deep with quicksand and a very strong current. We got to the other side, dismounted, tightened our saddle girths, and then swung into the saddles. When we got to the timber some of the men laid down and others knelt down. We got the skirmish line formed, and here the Indians made their first charge. There were 500 of them coming from the direction of the village. They were well mounted and well armed. They tried to cut through our skirmish line. We poured volleys into them, repulsing their charge.

Lt. Hodgson walked up and down along the line, encouraging the men to keep cool and lie low. Finally, when they could not cut through us, they strung out in single file, lying one side of their ponies from us and commenced to circle. They overlapped our skirmish line on the left and were closing in on our rear to complete the circle.

We had orders to fall back to our horses. This was where the first man was shot, Sgt. Miles F. O'Hara. He was a corporal going out on the expedition and was promoted sergeant a few days before his death. We found his head, with the heads of two other men, tied together with wire and suspended from a lodge pole in one of the Indian lodges, with all the hair singed off.

I looked in the rear in the direction of the river and saw the Indians completing the circle riding through the brush. I mentioned it to Captain French. He replied, "Oh, no, those are General Custer's men." Just on the moment, one of those Indians fired, and Private George Lorentz of my company was shot, the bullet striking him in the back of the neck, coming out of his mouth. He tipped forward out of his saddle.

Just then, the Indians fired into us in good shape. Major Reno rode up and said, "Any of you men who wish to escape, follow me." The order was given to charge, and away we went up the steep bank charging through the Indians in a solid body, Major Reno being in advance. As we cut through, the fighting was hand-to-hand, and it was death to anyone who fell from his horse or was wounded and was not able to keep up the command. The Indians were in great force on all sides of us. In this charge, there were about thirty men killed, but we reached the river. Bloody Knife, chief of scouts, also Charlie Reynolds, a white scout, and Isaiah Dorman, Negro interpreter, were killed. Lt. Hodgson was wounded and Lt. Donald McIntosh was killed. McIntosh was a half-breed Cherokee Indian and a brave and faithful officer.

Some dozen men became separated from the command and hid themselves in brush or in the woods or under the river embankment, and some of these men told me afterward that they stood in water up to their necks to keep out of sight of the Indians.

At this point, the river was about fifty yards wide with a swift current. Lt. Hodgson asked one of the men to carry him, his horse being shot and he being wounded. A trumpeter of my company, named Charles Fisher, better known as Bounce, told him to hold on to his stirrup and the horses drew [him] across the river. He was shot the second time and killed.

The opposite bank of the river was very steep, and the only way to get up to the bluffs was through a buffalo trail worn at the bank and only wide enough to let one man pass through at a time. Before we crossed the river, the fighting was desperate, and at close quarters. In many instances, the soldiers would fire the revolvers right into the breast of the Indians, and after their pistols were emptied some were seen to throw their revolvers away and grab their carbines. The Indians were about ten to one of us.

In scaling the bluffs, Dr. James DeWolf, a contract surgeon on the expedition, was killed. Also Sgt. Clair, and more. Their bodies with a number of others lay under cover of our guns, so the Indians did not get a chance to scalp them. After we gained the bluffs, we could look back and could see them, stripping and scalping our men and mutilating their bodies in a horrible manner. The prairie was all afire.

I counted as many as thirty arrows shot into one man's body and left there. It appears that some of the Indians sat on their horses and used their lances. We could not tell who many of the men were. If their uniforms had been on we probably could. Their bodies were scattered over the battlefield probably one and one half miles square. In burying the last of the men, we came to a gravel knoll, and here we found the body of general Custer. He was shot in two places; one bullet striking him in the right side of the face. The general was not scalped.

I served through the Civil War and saw many hard sights on the battlefield, but never saw such a sight as I saw there.

Little House on the Prairie

An excerpt

By Laura Ingalls Wilder

In one day Mr. Edwards and Pa built those walls as high as Pa wanted them. They joked and sang while they worked, and their axes made the chips fly.

On top of the walls they set up a skeleton roof of slender poles. Then in the south wall they cut a tall hole for a door, and in the west wall and the east wall they cut square holes for windows.

Laura couldn't wait to see the inside of the house. As soon as the tall hole was cut, she ran inside. Everything was striped there. Stripes of sunshine came through the cracks in the west wall, and stripes of shadow came down from the poles over-head. The stripes of shade and sunshine were all across Laura's hands and her arms and her bare feet. And through the cracks between the logs she could see stripes of the prairie mixed with the sweet smell of cut wood.

Then, as Pa cut away the logs to make the window hole in the west wall, chunks of sunshine came in. When he finished, a big block of sunshine lay on the ground inside the house.

Around the door hole and the window holes, Pa and Mr. Edwards nailed thin slabs against the cut ends of the logs. And the house was finished, all but the roof. The walls were solid and the house was large, much larger than the tent. It was a nice house.

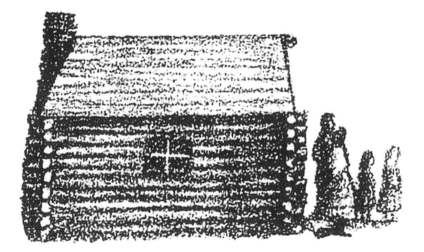

Hiawatha's Fishing

An excerpt

By Henry Wadsworth Longfellow

Forth upon the Gitche Gumee,
On the shining Big-Sea-Water,
With his fishing line of cedar,
Of the twisted bark of cedar,
Forth to catch the sturgeon Nahma,
Mishe-Nahma, King of Fishes,
In his birch canoe exulting
All alone went Hiawatha

Through the clear, transparent water
He could see the fishes swimming
Far down in the depths below him;
See the yellow perch, the Sahwa,
Like a sunbeam in the water,
See the Shawgashee, the crawfish
Like a spider on the bottom,
On the white and sandy bottom.

At the stern sat Hiawatha,
With his fishing line of cedar;
In his plumes the breeze of morning
Played as in the hemlock branches;
On the bows, with tail erected,
Sat the squirrel, Adjidaumo;
In his fur the breeze of morning
Played as in the prairie grasses.

On the white sand of the bottom
Lay the monster Mishe-Nahma,
Lay the sturgeon, King of Fishes;
Through his gills he breathed the water,
With his fins he fanned and winnowed,
With his tail he swept the sand-floor.

Cat's in the Cradle

By Harry Chapin

And the cat's in the cradle
And the silver spoon,
Little boy blue
And the man in the moon.

The Central Mountain of the World

By Black Elk

I saw myself on the central mountain of the world,
The highest place and I had a vision because
I was seeing in the sacred manner of the world.
The sacred mountain is Harney Peak in South Dakota.
And then I say, "But the central mountain is everywhere."

Cheyenne Warrior Nation Trilogy

By Lance Henson

1.
from the mountains we come
lifting our voices for the beautiful
road you have given

we are the buffalo people
we dwell in the light of our father sun
in the shadow of our mother earth

we are the beautiful people
we roam the great plains without fear
in our days the land has taught us oneness
we alone breathe with the rivers
we alone hear the song of the stones

2.
oh ghost that follows me
find in me strength to know the wisdom
of this life

take me to the mountain of my grandfather
i have heard him all night
singing among the summer leaves

3.
great spirit make me whole
i have come this day with my spirit
i am not afraid
for i have seen in vision
the white buffalo
grazing the frozen field
which grows near full circle
of this world

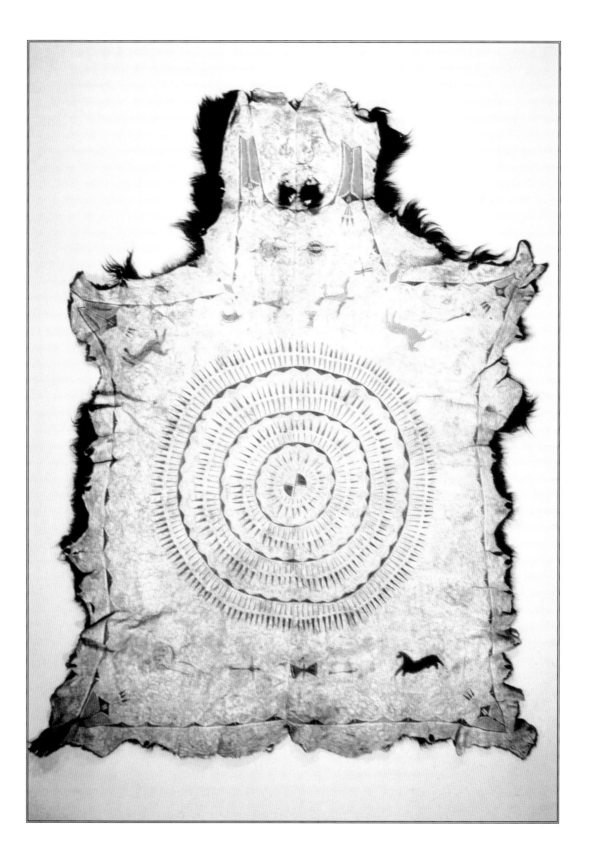

Back in the Saddle Again

By Gene Autry

I'm back in the saddle again, out where a friend is a friend—
Where the longhorn cattle feed on the lowly gypsum weed;
Back in the saddle again.
Ridin' the range once more; totin' my old .44—
Where you sleep out every night, and the only law is Right
Back in the saddle again.

She'll Be Coming Round the Mountain

An excerpt

Anonymous

She'll be coming round the mountain when she comes,
She'll be coming round the mountain when she comes,
She'll be coming round the mountain,
She'll be coming round the mountain,
She'll be coming round the mountain when she comes.

Oh, we'll all go down to meet her when she comes,
Oh, we'll all go down to meet her when she comes,
Oh, we'll all go down to meet her,
Oh, we'll all go down to meet her,
Oh, we'll all go down to meet her when she comes.

Rocky Raccoon

By John Lennon and Paul McCartney

Now somewhere in the black mountain hills of Dakota
There lived a young boy named Rocky Raccoon.
And one day his woman ran off with another guy.
Hit young Rocky in the eye.
Rocky didn't like that.
He said, "I'm gonna get that boy."
So one day he walked into town
Booked himself a room in the local saloon.

Rocky Raccoon checked into his room
Only to find Gideon's Bible.
Rocky had come equipped with a gun
To shoot off the legs of his rival.
His rival it seems had broken his dreams
By stealing the girl of his fancy.
Her name was Magill and she called herself Lill
But everyone knew her as Nancy.

Now she and her man who called himself Dan
Were in the next room at the hoedown.
Rocky burst in and grinning a grin
He said Danny boy this is a showdown
But Daniel was hot—he drew first and shot
And Rocky collapsed in the corner.

Now the doctor came in stinking of gin
And proceeded to lie on the table.
He said, "Rock, you met your match."
And Rocky said, "Doc, it's only a scratch
And I'll be better, I'll be better, Doc,
as soon as I am able."

Now Rocky Raccoon he fell back in his room
Only to find Gideon's Bible.
Gideon checked out and he left it no doubt
To help with good Rock's revival.

John Henry

An excerpt

Anonymous

When John Henry was a little baby
Sitting on his papa's knee,
Well, he picked up a hammer
And a little piece of steel,
Said, "Hammer's gonna be
The death of me, Lord, Lord,
Hammer's gonna be the death of me,
This hammer's gonna be the death of me
Lord, Lord, hammer's gonna be
The death of me."

The Days of '49

An excerpt

Anonymous

I'm old Tom Moore from the bummer's shore in the good ol' golden days
Call me a bummer and a ginsot, too, but what care I for praise
I wander around from town to town just like a roving sign,
And the people all say, "There goes Tom Moore of the days of forty-nine."

My comrades they all loved me well, a jolly saucy crew
A few hard cases I will admit, though they were brave and true.
Whatever the pinch they ne'er would flinch, they'd never fret or whine;
Like good ol' bricks they stood the kicks in the days of forty-nine.

Of all the comrades that I've had there's none that's left to boast,
And I'm left alone in my misery like some poor wandering ghost;
And as I pass from town to town they call me the rambling sign,
"There goes Tom Moore, a bummer shore, of the days of forty-nine."

Rawhide!

By Ned Washington and Dimitri Tiomkin

Rollin' rollin' rollin'

Keep movin' movin' movin'
Though they're disapprovin'
Keep them dogies movin'
Rawhide!
Don't try to understand 'em
Just rope and throw and brand 'em
Soon we'll be living high and wide.
Boy my heart's calculatin'
My true love will be waitin',
Be waitin' at the end of my ride.

Rollin' rollin' rollin'
Rollin' rollin' rollin'
Rollin' rollin' rollin' Rawhide!

Though the streams are swollen
Keep those dogies rollin'
Rawhide!
Rain and wind and weather
Hell-bent for leather

Wishin' my gal was by my side.
All the things I'm missin',
Good vittles, love, and kissin',
Are waiting at the end of my ride.

Move 'em on, head 'em up
Head 'em up, move 'em on
Move 'em on, head 'em up
Rawhide!
Count 'em out, ride 'em in
Ride 'em in, count 'em out
Count 'em out, ride 'em in
Rawhide!

Keep movin' movin' movin'
Though they're disapprovin'
Keep them dogies movin'
Rawhide!
My true love will be waitin',
Be waitin' at the end of my ride.
Rawhide!
Rawhide!

The Wells and Fargo Line vs. "Old Bill" Miner

By Roland Evers-Hoyt

Henry Wells and William G. Fargo, Easterners both, formed an express and freighting company in March 1852 to take advantage of the opportunities then burgeoning in California. They established a regular mail, package, and freight route between the East Coast and San Francisco. They set up branch lines to deliver mail and goods to California's far-flung gold-mining camps.

Much of what the company carried was money and gold dust, and the cargo made Wells Fargo wagons and coaches prime targets for robbery. Of the outlaws most notorious, one must certainly be identified: William "Old Bill" Miner. Miner ran away from home at the age of thirteen to become a cowboy, ended up in Southern California operating a mail service, and in 1869, tried his hand at robbing a Wells Fargo stagecoach. When his horse stumbled, he was captured, and he served a fifteen-year sentence in San Quentin. Released for good behavior, Miner teamed up with a highwayman named Bill Leroy and committed many stage and train robberies.

Miner spent a year traveling the world, returning to the States by 1880 to rob more stagecoaches. Apprehended in 1881, he served a twenty-year stretch in San Quentin. The middle-aged bandit was released in 1901 but continued to rob Wells Fargo coaches. In 1905, he was captured and sent to a Canadian penitentiary, from which he escaped [through a thirty-foot tunnel he patiently excavated] in 1907. "Old Bill" robbed a Portland, Oregon, bank in 1909 and a train near White Sulphur, Georgia, in 1911. Captured after this job, he was sentenced to life imprisonment. He broke out three times and was recaptured three times, declaring at last: "I guess I'm getting too old for this sort of thing."

Red River Valley

An excerpt

By James Kerrigan

From this valley they say you are going;
We will miss your bright eyes and sweet smile,
For they say you are taking the sunshine
That has brightened our pathway awhile.

Come and sit by my side if you love me.
Do not hasten to bid me adieu,
But remember the Red River Valley
And the cowboy that loves you so true.

Won't you think of this valley you're leaving?
Oh, how lonely, how sad it will be.
Oh, think of the fond heart you're breaking
And the grief you are causing me.

As you go to your home by the ocean
May you never forget those sweet hours
That we spent in the Red River Valley
And the love we exchanged 'mid the flowers.

BILLY THE KID
OUTLAW

Billy the Kid

By Alan Axelrod

Perhaps the most famous of all western gunfighters, Billy the Kid did not, in fact, kill the twenty-one men the song written about him credits him with. In sixteen documented gunfights, Billy killed four men. In the course of robberies, he may have assisted in killing an additional five.

Billy was born Henry McCarty in 1859. When his mother died of tuberculosis in 1874, Billy embarked on a career of petty crime, which soon escalated to murder when the seventeen-year-old killed a man in a saloon brawl. In 1878, Billy became embroiled in the so-called Lincoln County War, a feud between New Mexico cattlemen, in which he killed the sheriff of Lincoln County.

A fugitive now, Billy the Kid became a cattle thief and was hunted by Lincoln County's new sheriff, Pat Garrett, to whom he surrendered in December 1880. Four months later, however, Billy evaded the noose by killing his two jailhouse guards and escaping. Garrett ran him to ground at Fort Sumner, New Mexico, on July 14, 1881. Around midnight, Billy entered the adobe house of his supposed friend Pete Maxwell. "That's him," Maxwell said to Garrett, who had entered the house only a few minutes before. The sheriff fired twice at the dimly visible silhouette. The second shot went wild, but the first had found its mark, and Billy the Kid was dead.

Calamity Jane

By John Heard

Here the season of manifest destiny
And gold rush prairies.

Land-hungry time, Black-Jack time.

In each of us, an eye witness
Marthy Cannary, by herself

An eye witness

Born 1852, Missouri, oldest of six brats.
Rider until I became an expert rider.
able to ride the not rideable horse
overland to Virginia City,

Five-month journey, hunting the plains
or adventuring, shooting, and riding
way out beyond

many times crossed the Rockies
to Montana, our wagons
lowered over ledges, boggy places,
no use to be careful

Lost all, then there were dangers,
streams swollen; mounted a pony
to swim through currents and save
lives to amuse ourselves.

Ordered out to catch him
and cradle Hickok in my arms.
Christened me Calamity, heroine.

Deadwood, New Dakota
Derring-do boom-town
fallen into Silver Black Hills.

From Kingdom Come
Calam and Wild Bill
Parade down Main
Donned in buckskin, in beaver
Hammered golden, the sun;
and five hundred hombres.

Then to awaken on a familiar cot
and recall a stallion-tailed legend
"You're a wonderful little woman
to have around in time of calamity,"
says ol' Wild Bill when I save his life.

Hat Creek, Calamity Peak
crazed at Jake's Bar, fell in a lake.
Which animals befriend me?
the mule, the coyote, the cat:
stubborn, hunter, stray.

The real Calamity Jane for one dime only
my deeds and miscredits on far-off planets,
echoing eloquence toward oblivion.

They switch the date of death
to coincide with Bill's
and bury me by his side.

Pecos Bill Meets Paul Bunyan and Starts a New Ranch

By Leigh Peck

Even though Pecos Bill was boss of all the cowhands on the ranch, and had the very finest horse in all the world to ride, and had invented so many new things, he was not satisfied. He wanted to start a new ranch. A small place of just a few hundred thousand acres would do to begin with, he thought. Whenever he had a little time to spare, he rode out on Lightning [his horse] looking for a good place to start a ranch. In those days, there was plenty of land that anyone could have simply by claiming it. But Pecos Bill did not want just an ordinary ranch. He wanted the very best ranch in all the world.

Finally in Arizona he found the very piece of land that he was looking for, with grass taller than a man's head for the cattle to fatten on, creeks fed by springs of pure water for them to drink, and a few trees along the banks of the creeks, for shade in the heat of the day. The land was level except for one mountain. This mountain was tall and quite steep near the top. A very queer kind of birds, seen nowhere else in the world, made their nests among the rocks on the upper slopes of the mountain. They had to lay square-shaped eggs, because round eggs would have rolled right down the mountain.

Pecos Bill thought that this mountain would be just right for his headquarters ranch. The cattle could always find on it the climate they liked best. In cold days they could graze at the foot of the mountain, but in hot weather they could move up near the top, where it would always be cool. They could even have sunshine or shade, just as they wished, for one side of the mountain would be sunny while the other side was in the shade. It would not be likely to rain on both sides of the mountain at once, either, so the cattle could almost always keep dry. Certainly, the wind could not blow from more than one direction at once, and the cattle could always find a sheltered place where the wind was not blowing on them.

There was just one thing wrong with the mountain. It was covered with trees, huge tall trees, clear up to the rocky top. There was not room to ride a horse through the close-set trees, and certainly no room for cattle to graze there, or for grass to grow. Pecos Bill thought and thought, but he could not think of any way to clear the mountain of those trees. He hated to give up and admit there was anything that he could not do. Again and again he rode back to look at the mountain and try to figure out some way to clear it for his headquarters ranch.

Then one day, imagine his surprise and anger when he found someone else on his mountain! A hundred men were at work at the foot of the mountain putting up a big bunkhouse and a big cookhouse. They did not look like cowboys at all, and

126

they did not have any cattle with them, except for one huge blue-colored ox. He was a hundred times bigger than any steer Pecos Bill had ever seen before, and he ate a whole wagonload of hay at one swallow!

Pecos Bill did not stop to think that he was only one man against a hundred men, and that the huge ox could kill a man by stepping on him. He rode right up to the camp and asked, "Who is in charge here?"

"Paul Bunyan," answered one of the men.

"I want to talk to him," said Pecos Bill.

The man called "Paul" walked out from among the trees, the very biggest man in all the world—as big for a man as the Blue Ox was for a steer. Now Pecos Bill himself was a fine figure of a man, six feet two inches high, straight as an arrow and as strong and limber as a rawhide lariat. But this Paul Bunyan was so tall that his knee was higher than Pecos Bill's head! He had a long, dark beard. He wore flat-heeled, broad-toed boots, not like cowboy boots at all. He wore no chaps, and instead of a leather jacket he wore a queer woolen jacket of bright-colored plaid.

But if Pecos Bill was startled, he did not show it. He asked very firmly, "What are you doing on my mountain?"

"This is my mountain now," Paul Bunyan announced. "I've already settled on it."

"That makes no difference. I laid claim to this land long ago," Pecos Bill argued.

"Where's the law that says it's yours?" demanded Paul Bunyan.

"Here it is!" exclaimed Pecos Bill. "This is the law west of the Pecos."

"That's not fair!" cried Paul Bunyan. "I'm not armed. In the North Woods, we don't fight with pistols. We fight with our bare fists or with our axes."

"Very well," agreed Pecos Bill. "I'll give you the choice of weapons. I have no ax, but I'll use my branding iron to hit with."

Now the branding iron that Pecos Bill carried that day was what is called a running iron. It was only a straight iron bar with a crook on the end of it. Cowboys heat the end of a running iron and draw letters on a steer's hide as you would draw with a piece of crayon on paper.

Pecos Bill heated the end of his branding iron on a blazing star that he had picked up the time the stars fell. He always carried it about with him in his saddlebag, so as to have fire immediately whenever he needed one. Then the fight started.

Paul Bunyan hit at Pecos Bill so hard with his ax that he cut a huge gash in the earth. People call it the Grand Canyon of the Colorado River now.

Pecos Bill swung his red-hot iron, trying to hit Paul Bunyan, until the sands of the desert were scorched red-colored. That was the beginning of the Painted Desert out in Arizona.

Again Paul Bunyan tried to hit Pecos Bill and hit the ground instead. The queer rocks that are piled up in the Garden of the Gods in Colorado were split up by Paul Bunyan's ax in that fearful fight.

Pecos Bill's iron, instead of cooling off, got hotter and hotter, until the forests in New Mexico and Arizona were charred. These trees, burnt into stone by the heat from Pecos Bill's running iron, are called Petrified Forests now.

But neither man could get the better of the other. For the first and only time Pecos Bill had met his match. And it was the first and only time that Paul Bunyan's crew had seen a man that could stand up to him.

Finally they both paused to get their breath, and Paul Bunyan suggested, "Let's sit down and rest a minute."

"All right," agreed Pecos Bill, and they sat down on nearby rocks.

As they sat resting, Pecos Bill asked, "Stranger, why are you so anxious to take my land away from me? Isn't there plenty of other land in the West that you could have just by laying claim to it?"

"Land!" exclaimed Paul Bunyan. "It's not the land that I want!"

"Then why are we fighting? What do you want?" inquired the surprised Pecos Bill.

"Why, the trees, of course," Paul Bunyan explained. "I'm no rancher. I have no use for the land, any longer than it takes to get the timber off. I'll log the trees off that mountain, and then I'll be through with it. I'm a lumber man."

"Why didn't you say so at first?" exclaimed Pecos Bill. "You are more than welcome to the trees! I've been trying to find some way to get them off the land so that the grass can grow and my cattle can graze here."

"They'll be off in a few weeks," promised Paul Bunyan, and the two men shook hands.

Pecos Bill and Paul Bunyan were good friends after that, each respecting the other for the fight that he had put up. Pecos Bill had his cowboys drive over a herd of nice fat young steers to furnish beef for Paul Bunyan's loggers while they were clearing off the trees. When Paul Bunyan and his men were through, they left standing their bunkhouse and their cookhouse and the Blue Ox's barn, ready for Pecos Bill's outfit to move in.

On Top of Old Smoky

An excerpt

Anonymous

On top of Old Smoky, all covered with snow,
I lost my true lover, by courting too slow.

Well, courting's a pleasure, and parting a grief
But a false-hearted lover is worse than a thief.

A thief, he will rob you and take all you have,
But a false-hearted lover will send you to your grave.

They'll hug you and kiss you and tell you more lies
Than the cross ties on the railroad or the stars in the skies.

They'll tell you they love you just to give your heart ease,
And just as soon as your back's turned, they'll court whom they please.

I'll go back to Old Smoky, Old Smoky so high,
Where the wild birds and turtledoves can hear my sad cry.

Patches of Sky

By Debora Greger

Like a map blanketing a bed,
the flat fields slope enough so
under snow at sunrise some are coral,
some cornflower—cartographer's tints
taken from an old quilt.

Four hawks revolve over the square
where the wind has hollowed out a house,
and the next one, where it fills a tree

with feathered leaves, beaked cries.
Or so I say. Expansive for once,
I want to show you a countryside,
not a bed. Look—low hills folding
over centuries and at their base
someone's ragged crocuses
in what must have been a garden.

What the Lewis and Clark Expedition Began

Excerpt from Joseph Campbell's "The Power of Myth" lecture

What happened over two hundred years ago, when the Lewis and Clark Expedition inspired the white man to come West, was the beginning of the slaughter of the North American natives' animal of reverence.

This was a sacramental violation. You can see in many of the early eighteenth- and nineteenth-century paintings by George Catlin, of the Great Western Plains in his day, literally hundreds of thousands of buffalo all over the place. And then, through the next century, the frontiersman, equipped with repeating rifles, shot down whole herds, taking only the skins to sell and leaving the bodies there to rot. This was sacrilege.

It turned the buffalo from a "thou" to an "it."

The Indians had for decades addressed the buffalo as "thou," a being of reverence. Before the Lewis and Clark Expedition, the North American natives addressed all of life as a "thou"—the trees, the rivers, the clouds, everything. You can address anything as a "thou," and if you do it, you can feel the change in your own psychology. The consciousness that sees a "thou" is not the same consciousness that sees an "it."

Magic Words

Anonymous story from the coastal tribes

In the very earliest time,
when both people and animals lived on earth,
a person could become an animal if he wanted to
and an animal could become a human being.
Sometimes they were people
and sometimes animals
and there was no difference.
All spoke the same language.
That was the time when words were like magic.
The human mind had mysterious powers.
A word spoken by chance
might have strange consequences.
It would suddenly come alive
and what people wanted to happen could happen.
Nobody could explain this:
that's the way it was.

Ol' Man River

An excerpt

By Oscar Hammerstein and Jerome Kern

Ol' man river, dat ol' man river,
He must know sumpin', but don't say nothin',
He jus' keeps rollin', he jus' keeps on rollin' along.
He don't plant 'taters, he don't plant cotton,
An' dem dat plants 'em is soon forgotten,
But ol' man river, he jus' keeps rollin' along.

The Yellow Rose of Texas

An excerpt

Anonymous

There's a yellow rose of Texas I'm goin' for to see,
No other soldier knows her, nobody only me.
She cried so when I left her, it like to broke my heart,
And if I ever find her, we nevermore will part.

She's the sweetest rose of color this soldier ever knew.
Her eyes are bright as diamonds, they sparkle like the dew.
You may talk about your winsome maids and sing of Rosalie,
But the Yellow Rose of Texas beats the belles of Tennessee.

Refrain

Oh, I danced with the dolly
with a hole in her stocking
And her feet kept a-rocking and
her knees kept a-knocking
Oh, I danced with the dolly
with a hole in her stocking
And we danced by the light of
the moon.

Acknowledgments